EIGHT
OF
SWORDS

This book is dedicated to KPFA and the Pacifica Foundation network of radio stations for being the steadfast Voice of Progressive America since 1949. Warren Ritter listens faithfully, as do I.

ACKNOWLEDGMENTS

First there's the Minotaur/St. Martin's Press faction: P. J. Coldren, the reader for the Malice Domestic contest who loved my manuscript; Ruth Cavin, the best editor any mystery author could want; and John Cunningham, VP and associate publisher, who handed me my prize—you all changed my life. Then there were my presubmission editors, Laura Kennedy and Maryellen Johnson, who were instrumental in crafting this book, and my super agent, Jennifer Jackson. I acknowledge my great family: my daughter, Heather, who is carrying the beacon of social justice into the next generation; my parents, Jerry and Sally, my biggest fans; and my precious wife, Marla, who never wavered in her belief in me.

EIGHT
OF
SWORDS

CHAPTER ONE

Don'cha know, baby, I'm the one you need? Don'cha, don'cha, baby?"

The ebony '89 Cadillac Coupe Deville sported tinted windows, thick whitewalls, and gold trim that sparkled in the early afternoon sun. Its bass speakers echoed down the street. My client looked up and lip-synched along with "phat gangsta." She didn't hear me turn over the last card and say, "Oh, Jesus!"

Reading the tarot is a gig I do on Friday afternoons and weekends so that I don't have to say, "That blouse looks perfectly delightful on you!" My previous job was a two-year stint on the floor of the Nordstrom Correctional Facility. Working curbside on Berkeley's Telegraph Avenue was a real change of pace. Scabby dogs pissed on the legs of my card table. Schizophrenics, smelling like outhouses, hurled prophecies at me. I'd been hit with half-empty beer cans, bird droppings, and golf ball-size hailstones.

Still, it pays the bills. I can clear $100 on a sunny day. Most of the time I rattle off this fortune-telling jive without paying too much attention to what I'm saying. One reading blends into another. Clients don't care how articulate I am. They just want to know when they're going to win the lottery or if they're going to get laid.

I'd been working this corner for six years. Traffic noise, rap music, fire sirens, psychotic gibberish—nothing bothered me that much anymore. What bothered me right now were this chick's cards. Sometimes the cards reach up and grab me by the throat. The spread in front of me was screaming that my client was heading straight for Armageddon.

She'd walked up to my table and said, "Hi. My name's Heather. My stepdad thinks you're all a bunch of charlatans and con artists."

"Sit down, Heather. My name's Warren. Let's find out if he's right."

She said, "I'm game, I hate the SOB anyway. How much does it cost?"

Heather was on a shopping trip, passing my table on her way to the Gap. She was maybe sixteen, slightly overweight, decked out in a suede mini and a tight gray T-shirt with "Girls Football Number 29" printed on it. The lettering matched the green of her skirt and the green of her eyes. Her forest-green knapsack and taupe fanny pack coordinated with the rest of her outfit. Her short brunette hair was loaded with mousse and spiked to look like Tank Girl. She was dressed for a manageable adventure.

Heather told me her mom was into "all that psychic shit," but it just wasn't her thing. She'd never used tarot cards before. She'd sat down here for the fun of it. Fun? Not this reading.

She wanted to know about her boyfriend. I'd laid out the first set of four cards in a ten-card figure eight relationship spread. The beginning of the reading was dull normal.

"The first card is the Knight of Pentacles. A shrewd man with a dark complexion is coming into your life."

She giggled, nodded, and said, "That's my boyfriend."

Reading the tarot is 90 percent observation and 10 percent inspiration. I already knew a lot about Miss Heather. I knew she was from out of town. She wasn't decked out in Berkeley grunge. Below the waist, any Berkeley girl her age, rich or poor, will be dressed in ripped jeans and sneakers. She wasn't from San Francisco, either. I knew that for two reasons; girls from the city don't come here to shop, and her miniskirt wasn't black.

It was a chilly noon on Telegraph. The fog had just burned off. But Miss H. was wearing Alice Roi wrap-up gladiator-style sandals, and her toes had dark green polish on them. Her mini looked fresh off the rack of some nouveau boutique. I'd deduced that she dressed this morning in a balmier climate. She was slumming it in Berkeley, a tourist from some upscale white suburb in Contra Costa County, the sunny nirvana on the other side of the hills.

She'd laughed at me when I called the person dark complexioned. Why? I guessed that he might be black. Another confirmation that she wasn't from around here. Interracial dating is commonplace in the politically correct East Bay. She wouldn't dare giggle about his skin color. But it was still risqué and daring to be in a mixed relationship in the well-heeled boondocks.

A woman wants a reading about her boyfriend for two reasons—either to find out if he's cheating on her or to find out how devotedly he loves her. Heather looked cheery, so I picked door number two. Time to take a chance. If I was right, I'd look like a wizard. If I was wrong, I'd improvise.

"In fact, your boyfriend is black, and I can see from the next card, the Five of Wands, that there is opposition from your parents about this new relationship."

She was shocked and delighted. I'd batted a thousand. "God, you're really good. Both my mom and my stepdad hate his guts. How did you do that?"

I tried to look wise and mysterious. "And the fact that his card is next to the Page of Cups indicates that he is successful in the world but a bit naive in the ways of the heart." What young man isn't? She nodded.

Then I laid out the next three cards, and the reading went to hell. One sinister Major Arcana card after another: the Tower, the Devil, the Hanged Man. It was clear to me that the Dark One had targeted her and was coming to get her. And I don't even believe in this New Age crap.

I got to the card representing her, the Eight of Swords. That's when I used God Jr.'s name in vain, just as the pimpmobile with its fifty-pound woofers went rapping past.

I placed that card in the center of the spread and waited for her to look back at me. I looked hard into her lovely emerald eyes. Was she ready for this?

"You have a problem here," I said. "You see this card? The whole spread revolves around it. Here, look at it." I picked up the Eight of Swords and handed it to her. It depicts a woman, bound and blindfolded, with eight long swords driven into the ground around her.

As she examined the card, she said, "Creepy!"

"This is what faces you in your immediate future. And the long-term outlook isn't much better. See." She followed where I was pointing and saw the Devil card: Lucifer was sitting on a throne that had a man and a woman chained to it. I went on,

"This theme of being restrained, tied down and bound, runs all through this spread. What do you think it means?"

Her brow wrinkled and she frowned. It didn't look like she was having a lark. Before she could respond, I heard the opening notes of Bach's Toccata and Fugue in G minor coming from her lap. "Shit, just a sec," she said, zipped open her fanny pack, and pulled out a stuffed animal that looked like a blue Eeyore. She flipped it over, punched a button, and held it to her ear. That's when I figured out it was a cutesy cell phone cover.

"Hi, Mom. Yeah, I'm fine. I'm in Berkeley. Hey, you should be happy, I'm getting my cards read. . . . Yes, I'm alone! Mom, give it a rest will you! . . . Sure, I'll be home by then. Okay, later." She turned off the donkey phone and stuffed it back into her pouch.

"Okay, where were we? Oh, yeah, being tied down. I think it's about my stepdad. He's a total control freak. He started out so sweet. I thought he was the coolest. I was so wrong! He adopted me and made me take his last name: Wellington. Gross! What a preppy name. And that was just the beginning. I had to sign a will, and then he registered the car that my real dad left me in his name. He picks out the clothes he wants me to wear. He reviews my homework before I turn it in. And he's a fossil when it comes to dating. I mean, he believes in curfews. He waits at the door when I come home after a date, all ready with the inquisition. He is positively *prehistoric!*"

I didn't think Dad's dating rules had anything to do with her oncoming cataclysm. It looked more like she was just about to get strapped down on the Amtrak railroad tracks and run over by the San Joaquin Express. But there's a limit to what I say to cute young clients. I wasn't going to call her a liar. I turned over the ninth card. Whew, light at the end of the tunnel. I decided to end her reading one card early.

"The last card in your spread is Strength. In terms of your relationship with your boyfriend, the image of a goddess gently opening the mouth of a lion represents the reality that you have the upper hand with him. You can call the shots. Am I right?"

She nodded. "I know, he's so sweet. Not like my last boyfriend. Curtis, Curly is my name for him, he always wants to know what I want. I think he's the nicest guy I've ever known. But you're right, he does follow my lead, thank goodness!"

I went on, "This card also stands for the strength you have inside you, strength you'll need to face everything that will be coming your way." I picked up one of my address labels and pasted it on the bottom of the Eight of Swords card. This was a marketing trick I learned years ago. I used it to end all my sessions. I liked that the card was so big that a client felt bad about tossing it away. I heard that they often ended up on people's home altars. Great advertising.

I told Heather, "Here, I want you to take this card with you and know that whatever befalls you, it will ultimately turn out all right. My phone number and e-mail are on the label on the bottom of the card. Contact me if you want to set up a private tarot session in a few weeks to find out more about how these patterns are about to play themselves—"

A sharp blast of a horn interrupted me. "Hey, Heather Feather, how do you like your Mister Chocolate Sundae Motherfucker?" A tall, chunky white guy in his midtwenties was hanging out of the window of a silver Pontiac Grand Am. He was wearing a blue bandanna and a T with sleeves cut off and a picture of a rabid rodent holding an AK-47 on it. A gangster wannabe.

Heather looked up and said, "Shit!" under her breath. She never broke eye contact from the jerk yelling at her while she whispered to me, "Speak of the devil. That's Hal, my ex." Then she stood up and gave him the finger. Go, Tank Girl.

The cretin yelled back, "Yeah, well, fuck you, too. You going to fuck this old fortune-teller? You fuck everything else that wears pants." I could see why he was an ex-boyfriend.

I was just about to act like a jerk right back at him when the light turned green and he sped off, laying rubber and waving his outstretched middle finger at both of us. Heather sighed. "You know, sometimes it feels like he's stalking me. He comes by and dumps shit on me at the weirdest times. He lives in Concord. What's he doing here?"

I said, "I wish he'd been on foot. I'd have enjoyed teaching him a few things about proper manners toward women and his elders."

"Not a good idea, Warren. He's really mean, and the gang he runs with is worse. They're into pretty heavy things—drugs, guns, maybe even gang rape, but Hal always denied that one. Stay away from him. Anyway, Warren, thanks for the reading. It was really good, a lot more right on than I expected." She took my card, stuck it in her backpack, tossed a twenty on the table, and hurried off.

I opened my backpack and riffled through a big pile of cards until I found another Eight of Swords. I slipped it into the deck on the table. I carried around about a dozen loose packs of tarot cards with me. It always impressed clients when I did the give-them-the-card trick. I had snagged a lot of private sessions that way.

But I doubted that I'd ever see Heather again. That reading had been too heavy for her. Out of curiosity I turned over the last card in her spread, the one I had avoided looking at while she was there. There was a skull looking out of the helmet of his black armor, riding his chalky horse right toward Heather Wellington.

There's a coldness that descends in the presence of Death. No one wants to be around it. We move away, avert our glance, occupy ourselves somewhere else. In medieval times, people were more direct. They held up crucifixes, genuflected, or made their fingers into the shape of the cross to ward off the Reaper. At least these gestures gave them something to do besides shiver and feel sick.

I wanted to pretend that I didn't know what was slouching toward Heather. After all, there was nothing I could do about it. Right?

CHAPTER TWO

*A*ll right, Warren, you're under arrest for doing business without a valid permit, obstructing the sidewalk, and conspiracy to defraud a minor."

I spoke without looking up. "Don't worry, Mac, she was from Contra Costa County."

"Oh, well, go ahead and fleece the shit out of her, then," said Officer James McNally.

He was my favorite cop, in fact the only cop I could stomach. Mac was in his late twenties, with a wiry build, unruly brown hair, close-set gray-blue eyes, and a permanent five-o'clock shadow.

He looked a bit ridiculous in his blue Bermuda shorts, astride his bicycle. Mac, a proud member of the Berkeley Bike Squad of the BPD, was riding what looked to be a Trek cross-country bike. He'd let me in on the truth. It was a Ventana Pantera custom-made frame with X-dream Superlite components. Maybe $4,500 worth of bike.

We'd met two years ago at the Bull's-eye Precision Indoor

Shooting Range in Marin. We both carried Kimber Team Match II .45s. I bet him a dinner at Tandoori Chicken USA that I could outshoot him. My eighty-three beat his seventy-nine, and we stuffed ourselves on Indian fast-food take-out. It wasn't until we were well into our second order of pakoras that he told me he was a cop. Feeling victorious and well fed, I forgave him this slight transgression and set up another time for us to go shooting.

We met once a month or so at the Bull's-eye to compete. He was a good shot, and I bought my share of dinners. He was as close as I allowed a male friend to get.

I said, "The cards tell me I'm due for two Tandoori chicken sandwiches, an order of veggie pakoras, and a pint of Foster's. When can you come to Bull's-eye and get humiliated?"

"Not this Friday, but next, at eleven. Hey, I'd love to chat, but I've got to get rolling. My sergeant is on my butt these days. Too much fraternizing with the natives, not enough law enforcement. See you in Marin. Bring your wallet."

As he kicked off, cut across the steady stream of one-way traffic, and headed down the Ave toward the university I shouted after him, "Get a real job. Rob banks!"

CHAPTER THREE

R ichard! Is that you?"

It was late in the day. I was just beginning what was going to be my last reading. It was for one of my steady clients, a social worker who came to me for advice about some of the more loony clients she worked with at a local homeless shelter. Suddenly, an all too familiar voice intruded into our reading.

I looked up and saw my sister crossing the street toward me, looking very perplexed. My stomach seized up. Shit, at last it happened. After thirty years, someone from my past saw through my plastic surgery and recognized me. She could blow my whole life apart. I leaned over the table and spoke in a confidential tone, "Helen, my schizophrenic sister is coming over here. I guess she sneaked out of her halfway house again. Whenever she does that, she always tracks me down. Here's your money. We'll have to do this reading at another time. I've got to get her back before she gets in trouble."

Helen nodded sympathetically. She knew this type of problem well. Then Tara stood over us.

"Excuse me, are you Richard Green? Your laugh sounds just like him, and you sit like he did. But no, you look different. Besides, he's dead." She leaned forward as though she was peering into me. "Richard, is that you? Oh, my God! It is you!"

I nodded to Helen. We were obviously in the presence of a lunatic. My own sister was calling me by another name. What more evidence would anyone need?

I folded up my table as I said to Tara, in a soothing voice, "Don't worry, Tara. Everything is going to work out fine. Just help me get this stuff put away and we can go somewhere and talk."

Tara said, "It couldn't be. You, how dare you! You wouldn't have done something like that! Where the hell have you been for the past thirty years?"

I turned from Tara and surreptitiously rolled my eyes at my client. Helen asked me, "Are you okay, Warren? Are you going to need any help?"

I answered, "No, I don't need your help, but thanks, anyway. Everything's under control. Maybe next week, okay?"

She nodded and walked off. Tara had escalated to DEFCON three, "What's with this 'Warren' crap, Richard? And I'm sure as hell *not* under control. You have some explaining to do, mister!"

I kept ignoring my sister, packing away my cards and sign until Helen was out of earshot. Then I turned on Tara and in an intense whisper said, "Look, sis, shut the fuck up, or you're going to get me in a shitload of trouble. I'll explain everything, but *not here*. Now grab this table and help me cart this stuff to the back room of this bookstore. And stop calling me Richard!"

Tara relaxed. I was acting like an asshole. This was more like the guy she'd been raised with. She said, "Fine, Richar—I mean whatever your name is now. You schlep your own damn table. I'll wait right here. But move it. You're thirty years late."

I had an arrangement with Cody's, the bookstore by the corner where I worked. I could store my sign, chairs, table, and bag of tarot cards in their back room for a minimal fee. It was a good deal for them because I rarely got out of there without buying a book.

As I went in, I just wanted to keep on going right past the "Staff Only" sign, out the back door, down the alley, and away from my past. The only reason I was still alive was that no one knew my real name. Now my big sister was broadcasting it to the world. But I knew that if I disappeared, she might raise a big enough stink to catch the attention of the FBI.

No, she had to be managed, not dumped. I was never very good at controlling her as a kid. I hoped I'd learned a few skills since then.

Tara had been Daddy's girl, a testy redhead with freckles on perpetually sunburned skin. Except for her father, Tara never liked human beings very much. She loved animals, the wilder the better. People annoyed her, and she let them know that. That attitude was about to be turned on me full force.

I looked at her through the bookstore window before going back out to encounter her. The past three decades had taken their toll on her. She was pale. Her hair was still auburn, a good dye job with blond streaks professionally added. I noticed the deep crow's-feet around her eyes, her furrowed brow, and a nervous habit of continually scanning the street.

I came out and took her arm, trying for a jolly approach. "Let's talk later, sis. Right now I'm starving. Tara, you're in gourmet heaven. Name a country and I'll find a restaurant around here with its food."

She said, "Philadelphia."

I smiled, "You're lying, you hate fast food. But IB's Hoagies and Cheesesteak Shop is right down the street, on Durant."

She smiled, too. I remembered that smile. A nine-year-old boy inside of me sparked up, and I thought, *Hey, there's my sister!* The tiniest wetness welled into my eyes. What a price I'd paid when I cut off myself from her.

She said, "You're right. I hate hoagies. Make it Ethiopian food."

She'd always been drawn to Africa. She'd been planning to do a junior year sabbatical studying elephants in the Chobe River Valley in Botswana the year that I "died."

"We want The Blue Nile, then, three blocks south. Look, there's a lot I need to tell you, but not over dinner where anyone can eavesdrop. And please keep your very dramatic voice down."

She glared at me. I went on, "Now, I know you hate taking orders, but if you won't play by these rules, I have to leave right now. I'm not being a macho pig. You've got to trust me on this. Deal?"

I expected a scathing counteroffer, but she just looked at me with that fuck-with-me-and-you-die look and said, "Barely."

Telegraph was getting ready for the night. Vendors were striking their racks of crystals, pipes, cheap Indian jewelry, and T-shirts. The energy was shifting from busy hippie commercialism to the loneliness of the evening. Everyone got edgier and needier as the sun went behind the funky office buildings that lined the Ave.

The restaurant looked like the set for a sixties summer-of-love movie: bead curtains, dark blue walls, low lighting, international incomprehensible music. It was the perfect place to spark up a doobie and feed your munchies. The entrée was served on top of a disk of spongy bread. You wrapped the bread around bites of your dinner. No silverware; you ate by hand. Tough on the laundry bill but easy on the dishwasher.

The conversation was minuscule. Tara said, "I'm not going to say anything about myself until you're able to explain how you get blown up in the seventies, we have a funeral for you, and then you show up as a fortune-teller thirty years later."

Silence descended. It was a meditative meal. We were able to savor every bite without constant conversational interruptions. However, my inner conversation was terrified! How much can I tell her? How much can I trust her? Will she catch me if I lie? She was always good at that when we were kids, but I'd had a lot of practice since then. I decided on a story that was pretty close to the truth. I finished my dinner with no memory of what the food tasted like.

Tara announced abruptly, "I need to go. Let's get out of here," and got up. I tossed $40 on the table and ran out to catch up with her.

Once we hit the streets, she started right in, "Look, Richard—and don't tell me that's not your damn name. I picked it out. I convinced Mom and Dad to name you that. If it wasn't for me, you'd be named Rhett. I don't want to wait till we're sitting around in your crash pad. I want to know right now. What happened?"

"Look, sis, it wasn't anything I really planned. It just sort of started happening, and I couldn't really stop it. What happened is—"

She stopped me. "You're getting ready to lie to me. Shit, Ricky, you think I'm stupid? I know you. Goddamn you! I can't do this. I'm so mad I just want to run you over. I'm not going to trot over to your goddamn apartment and get lied to, or even get told the truth to. I've had it! I just want to scream. How the hell could you do this to your mother, your father, your girl-friend . . . Oh Christ, what am I going to do about that!"

"Do about what?" I asked.

"None of your goddamn business! Because you're dead. You've been dead for thirty years. And I'll regret to my dying day taking this professorship at Cal and finding my lying brother as a street person."

"I'm not a—" I didn't get very far.

She slapped me across the face. "Just shut up! I'm going home now. We're not going to talk until you're ready to tell me the truth. And you're not ready to do that, are you?"

She'd nailed me. I shook my head. I hadn't told anyone the whole truth, and I sure as hell wasn't going to start with her.

She said, "I don't know when or where we'll have our little chat. But it sure isn't going to be tonight. If I want to talk to you, I know where to find you: doing psychic readings on your lowlife friends. Don't you dare say one more word, RICHARD GREEN, asshole!" She shouted that name as loudly as she could. Then she stomped off toward the university.

Since we were practicing inappropriate behavior, I shouted after her, "Call me, Tara! My voice mail is 1-800 TAROT-MAN." She gave me no sign that she was listening.

That didn't go very well. I looked around. No one seemed to have noticed our scene. Ever since Reagan shut down the mental hospitals, minidramas much worse than this happened every day on the Ave. That's why they call Berkeley "the open ward."

Still, I was glad I didn't recognize anyone. That name she was screaming had been extinguished, buried under tons of rubble years ago. If it flared up again and started to spread, it could become a firestorm, and I was the one who would be immolated.

CHAPTER FOUR

I wasn't ready to go home. My face still stung. I felt like shit. I had to walk it off. I headed north on a rambling course through the campus.

The sun had set. Street lamps failed to push back the growing darkness. Steam rose from vents in the sidewalk, giving the walk a moody, London feel. I smelled freshly cut grass. One deep peal from the bell tower announced 9:30. Then silence reformed around me. The quiet was broken once by the *whoosh whoosh* sound of a bicyclist speeding past me, hurling himself down a tiny valley and out of sight. I took a deep breath and unwound a couple of the knots in my belly.

I emerged from the university near North Shattuck, a neighborhood of bright lights, supermarkets, and gourmet restaurants. Autos honked, stoplights blinked, and people rushed from their cars to their favorite Thai restaurant. This was my turf.

I headed for Black Oak Books. Bookstores are always a refuge for me. It was almost closing time. A handful of customers wandered the overstocked aisles. I walked to the rear corner of the store to my favorite shelves: the poetry section.

I began pulling out books at random, flipping through them. I was hungry for a bit of solace before the clerks kicked me back out into the night.

I found what I needed in a well-worn copy of *Dream Work* by Mary Oliver. The book opened to a page that was dog-eared, with a small grease stain on one corner. I read:

THE JOURNEY

One day you finally knew
what you had to do, and began,
though the voices around you
kept shouting
their bad advice—
though the whole house
began to tremble
and you felt the old tug
at your ankles.
"Mend my life!"
each voice cried.
But you didn't stop.
You knew what you had to do,
though the wind pried
with its stiff fingers
at the very foundations—
though their melancholy
was terrible.
It was already late
enough, and a wild night,
and the road full of fallen
branches and stones.

But little by little,
as you left their voices behind,
the stars began to burn
through the sheets of clouds,
and there was a new voice,
which you slowly
recognized as your own,
that kept you company
as you strode deeper and deeper
into the world,
determined to do
the only thing you could do—
determined to save
the only life you could save.

The melancholy *was* terrible. Reading Oliver somehow helped. I'd done what I thought I had to do. Maybe I was wrong, but it was too late now to go back. I closed the book, returned it to the shelf, wiped the tear from my face, and headed back to my apartment.

As I strolled past La Val's Pizza, I glanced in. The pizza parlor has a giant-screen television fully visible from their front window. Tonight I was in no mood for a media fix. I just looked in for a moment as I passed and then looked away. I took another step before realizing what I had just seen. It was the face of the girl I did the reading for today, looking out at me from a high school photo. The caption over her picture said "Kidnapped!"

I spun around and ran in, just catching the tail end of the anchorwoman's commentary. "The police have just informed this station that they interviewed a woman who lives in a Berkeley halfway house. She reports seeing a young teenager matching Heather Wellington's description being forced into a white van on the corner of Bancroft and Telegraph at about noon.

"No one has heard from her since then. Her parents are offering a ten-thousand-dollar reward for information that may lead to her return. The Amber Alert child abduction warning system has been activated statewide.

"On your screen is the eight-hundred number of the Danville police hot line for the Heather Wellington case. If you have any information about this incident, or if you have seen her at any time today, please call immediately. No other details are available at this time, but stay tuned for an update tomorrow morning on the seven o'clock Sunrise News Hour.

"Now, on a lighter side, today turned out to be a lucky one for Rex, the gibbon ape that escaped from the Oakland Zoo last Thursday . . ."

Shit. Life just doesn't stop coming at you.

CHAPTER FIVE

Back on the Ave the next day, I couldn't get Heather out of my head. I kept seeing images of her being gang-raped, killed, chopped up and stuffed into a garbage bag. Sometimes my imagination is too fertile. I couldn't get away from the dark cards that had appeared in her reading, either. In every spread I did I kept getting the Devil, the Tower, the Eight of Swords, the Hanged Man, or Death. Sometimes the cards are like that. They keep recycling, tapping me on the shoulder until I get the message.

I hate it when the cards act like they have a life of their own. As I sat there waiting for the next client to show up, I wondered for the forty thousandth time, *What the hell am I doing here? What is a leader of the Weather Underground doing playing low-rent guru to the new millennium?*

In adolescence I had no Age of Aquarius leanings. I was a red, white, and blue Boy Scout. In college my focus shifted to red. Protesting social injustice and fighting the tyranny of capitalism eclipsed any other interests. Then, in the seventies, all I cared about was my physical survival.

The first time I ever saw a tarot deck was in Mexico. I was down there in 1972 getting cosmetic surgery to alter my appearance. It took a week to turn my Jewish nose aristocratic and remove the squirrel-like cheek pouches. Eyebrows got thinned and hair dyed and straightened. I ended up looking permanently hungry.

This wasn't vanity. I had to become unrecognizable. After the bandages came off and the bruises went down, I looked like a short, brown-haired, hazel-eyed, underfed Prince Charming.

During the six weeks I hung out in Mexico City waiting for the bruises to fade, I wandered around looking for good bars. One night I passed a tiny shop with a sign in its window in English. I stopped and read, "Tarot card readings. Your life has been all but wasted. It's not too late. Come inside, American tourist, and find out what can be done for your own redemption."

I was intrigued. I opened the door and entered a room lit by candles. There must have been almost a hundred of them, in all shapes and sizes. One candle was about a foot wide and two feet tall. At least fifty votive candles flickered in their multicolored glass containers, resting on a narrow, shoulder-high shelf encircling the room.

In the middle of the room stood a small wooden table and an empty dining-room chair. Behind the table sat the largest human being I'd ever seen. He was planted in a massive leather chair that couldn't quite hold him. He was white, bald, with fierce ebony eyes and chin after chin rippling down over his neck.

He spoke with a Southern accent. "Yes, I'm fat, I know. Go ahead, look me over. That way you don't have to peek at me out of the side of your eyes while you're talkin' to me." He lifted his sagging arms wide. I did what he suggested and let my eyes travel over his unbelievable girth.

After a moment I said, "Okay, I'm through looking. Tell me about your sign in the window."

He had a deep voice. "You don't believe in this psychic crap. You just came in here to kill time. I'm not going to make a peso off you. Sit down."

He had me pegged. To my surprise, I sat down anyway.

He went on, "My name is Philip. Watch."

His orangutan hands were surprisingly dexterous as he deftly manipulated his deck. I've never been able to find the deck he was using. It looked old. The edges of the cards were frayed. Several cards were torn or just worn through. Each card had been carefully remounted on thicker card stock to keep it from falling apart.

The pictures on the cards were from the Italian Renaissance period, but the images were surrealistic and disturbing. The perspectives were warped and the bodies distorted. It was as if the painter had been on a bad acid trip when he painted them.

Philip laid out ten cards faceup in a line. Then he turned them over and shuffled them back into the deck. He gently reshuffled the deck and laid out another line of ten cards. He did this four times. Any card that showed up twice, he placed aside. He had a prodigious memory for what had been laid down in the previous spreads.

By the time he was through, he had the nine cards put aside. These he placed facedown in front of him in a haphazard relationship. Then he began arranging them. First in a circle, then a box with cards forming an X inside the box, and finally as a figure eight.

He turned over the card at the top of the spread and the one on the bottom. The top card showed a jester juggling some balls, unaware he was just about to walk over a cliff. Philip said,

"That's one of your faces." The bottom card was a skeleton riding an emaciated horse. He touched it with his fat forefinger. "That's your other face." Then he turned over the card in the middle, the one that connected the two loops. On it a minaret was being struck by a lightning bolt. Flames spread up the sides of the structure. A man and a woman, hand in hand, leaped from the top balcony, about to plunge to their doom.

Philip moved his finger until it was hovering over the two falling figures and then looked at me and said, "You killed them."

I jumped up, knocking my chair over behind me. "Shut the fuck up!" I yelled and stormed out. I never wanted to see him again. He was much too close to the bone.

The next time I even thought about the tarot was six years ago. I was sick of my job at Nordstrom. I was ready for my next gig. Standing on a Berkeley street corner waiting for the light to change, I overheard the tarot card reader talking to the guy who sells T-shirts and bumper stickers advocating the legalization of marijuana. The tarot guy was saying, "Yep, Saul, one more week and I'm out of here. I'm heading to Montana to homestead. I'm not going to miss this freak show at all!"

Something clicked, and what came out of my mouth amazed me. I turned and asked him, "Excuse me, I just overheard what you were saying. I've always wanted to be more public with my tarot readings. How much would you want to sell your business for?"

He looked surprised. I imagine he'd never thought about selling his little enterprise. He looked down at his battered table, portable camp chairs, and Technicolor sign, and then looked back at me.

He said, "I have quite a stable of regular customers. That's worth a lot. But I might be willing to sell this enterprise, assuming you're a competent reader. The deal would include my ten years of sweat equity, my little black book of former and regular out-call clients, my Berkeley peddler's license, and everything you see here except my cards. It's worth at least a thousand dollars."

He sat back, getting ready for the counteroffer. I stunned him. I said, "Deal. I'll bring you five hundred cash next Saturday. At that time I'll do a couple of demonstration readings for you. If you're satisfied, I'll come by Sunday evening to get your book of addresses, your vendor's license, the table and the chairs. I'll give you the second five hundred then."

He smiled and agreed. I bet he thought he'd just pulled off his biggest con.

I went home, called in sick for next week's shift at Nordie, and started to study. This was just what I was looking for, a part-time, cash-only job where I was my own boss. Who knows, it might even be fun.

I bought a Rider-Waite deck of cards and seven books on the tarot. I filled a three-ring binder with sections for each card and took notes on all the different interpretations. I practiced laying out the different spreads: the Celtic Cross, the Tree of Life, the Horoscope, and the Chakra Spread.

I dialed 900 numbers every day to get tarot readings on the phone. I needed to listen to their delivery. I laid out a spread and then imagined using those cards with four different clients. How would I adapt the interpretations for a coed, a jock, a hippie, or a senior citizen? By Saturday, I'd crammed and was ready.

The final exam was a major disappointment. Ray, the tarot reader, was much more interested in my money than he was in my delivery. He had me do one sample session on him and then told me I was excellent and that he'd see me on Sunday with the rest of the cash.

Twenty-four hours later I was Telegraph's reigning tarot reader. There was just one problem. To have Ray's peddler's license switched over to my name, I'd have to get fingerprinted. That wouldn't work for me. As far as I knew, my fingerprints weren't in any database, and I wanted it to stay that way.

It cost me $250 to get a forged California driver's license with Ray's name on it and my picture. It wasn't top quality, but I was going to have to use it only once a year. In a sense, Ray never left Berkeley. Every year I'd go into the permit office and renew my peddler's license in his name, paying cash. They assumed I was Ray Stevens. The police saw the same sign and table in the same location and never checked to see whose name the permit was in. I was in business!

I still look on tarot reading as a branch of the entertainment industry. People pay me because they want to know that their life is going to work out all right. They're hoping against hope that one or two of their secret dreams might come to pass. My job is to read the clients more than I read the cards and to give them what they need: to guess their dream and validate it.

But Heather was right. Sometimes it is creepy. The cards don't care whether or not I believe in them. Each year I do this work, the cards get pushier and pushier. They keep repeating themselves, resisting randomness. They fall again and again in the same patterns and sequences, no matter how often I shuffle them.

On Sunday, my first reading included Death, Hanged Man, and the Eight of Swords. My second reading contained the Devil and the Tower. Third reading: Eight of Swords, Tower, Devil. This was damn annoying.

I don't believe there's a God the Father out there, consulting a long scroll of parchment to find out who's been naughty or nice. The universe doesn't care. Things happen for no reason at all. No one beats death, and nothing you can do can buy one more second. And that means no angels are out there working overtime to communicate with me.

So what the hell was happening with these cards? The odds were astronomical that the same cards would haunt me like this. By the fourth reading I'd strained coincidence past the breaking point.

I just wanted to yell at my spreads and say, "Will you shut up and leave me alone! There is nothing I can do about this situation. Give me a break!"

This behavior wouldn't raise an eyebrow on the Ave. People are constantly talking to walls, strangers, lampposts, or the sky. I'd just be one more nutcase. Which was how I felt.

CHAPTER SIX

Just because I don't work from nine to five, Monday
through Friday doesn't mean I'm a slacker. For an an-
archist, I have a disciplined daily routine. Up at 6:30
for twenty minutes of yoga stretches. Ten minutes of
meditative sitting (it keeps my blood pressure down).
Then a half hour of chores: Monday—muck out the kitchen,
Tuesday—clean the bathroom, Wednesday—vacuum and dust,
Thursday—do the laundry, Friday—day of rest. I'm half Jewish.

Today was Mop & Glow the kitchen day. There's something
artificially seductive about housework. When we're absorbed in
a task like laundry or dusting, we can pretend that what we're
doing is sufficient to justify our existence. After all, we're doing
our chores, being good boys and girls. Death won't take us if
we're good.

I'd read that medical patients who receive unexpected terminal diagnoses sometimes go into a fit of housecleaning. They're
trying to impose order and tidiness on a chaotic and ultimately
fatal universe.

The biggest lie of all happens when we're all done. We look

at that pile of folded clothing, or that shiny kitchen floor, and think, *There, it's done!* We hope that life will turn out like that, a series of simple tasks with clear beginnings, middles, and satisfactory endings.

The phone rang and disrupted my puny attempts to organize chaos. A man asked, "Is this Warren Ritter?"

"Yes."

"You're a tarot card reader?" he asked.

So far so good. "Yes."

"When did you last see Heather Wellington?"

Uh-oh. Hum, lie, or tell the truth? No telling who this guy was or how much he knew. When in doubt, lead with stupidity. "Who?"

The voice said, "I'd better introduce myself. I'm Detective Robert Flemish of the Danville Police Department. I'm investigating the kidnapping of Heather Wellington. She's a brunette teenager, normal height, green eyes, last seen Saturday afternoon on Telegraph Avenue wearing a green skirt and a gray T-shirt. Does that help jog your memory?"

I'd play the stupid hand to the end. "Look, Officer, I see thousands of teenagers every weekend. I can't say whether I remember . . ."

"We recovered her backpack in Oakland. She had your business card in it. Does that help?"

Oops. Time to shift strategies. "Oh, *that* Heather! I never knew her last name. Pudgy, and I think the shirt said something about girls' football?"

"That's the one," he said.

"Yeah, sure. She had a reading with me. Was it Saturday? Yes, it was! I remember her cards. A real mess, lots of negative Major Arcana. She was kidnapped?" Was I sounding ditzy enough?

"What time did you do your reading with her?"

Good old tactic, answer a question with a question. I was tempted to respond in kind, saying something like, "When did she get kidnapped?" But I thought better of it.

"Sometime early afternoon. After twelve and before three, I think. I'm not totally sure, I did a lot of readings that day."

"Please tell me anything out of the ordinary that happened in that reading."

Sure. Why not? I gave him the blow by blow. I hate pigs, but I didn't want to get dragged into the station for more questioning. I told him how her mom hated Heather's new boyfriend, who was black and named Curtis. How her father was controlling. How her ex-boyfriend Hal drove by and gave us the finger.

I fielded lots of questions about the car Hal was in, the nature of her relationship with Curtis, her state of mind. Yeah, right, like he thinks I'm a psychic or something? I did the best I could, considering that my armpits start to spit whenever I have to talk to a strange cop.

Finally he said, "Well, thank you for your assistance. Please let me know if you are planning to leave the area. I may have further questions for you."

"Sure." At least he didn't haul me in. Yet.

CHAPTER SEVEN

I've got one last question about your sister and then I want to move on to something else. I know I'm probably going to piss you off asking this, but that's my job. Are you sure you really met her, or could you just have imagined it, like you imagined that chase scene with FBI agents two years ago?"

I said, "You know, Rose, sometimes I really regret starting to work with you. Everything I say gets twisted around and thrown back at me. Yeah, sure, I was whacked out that time when I ran through Berkeley. You're right. I was convinced that the Tac squad was after me. But this is totally different. You want me to bring her in here to prove to you she exists? When are you going to start trusting me?"

"I trust you, Warren, and I ask hard questions. If I thought you were completely paranoid I'd never ask you those questions. I'm just checking things out. So here's my next concern. I think there's something else bothering you, something that has nothing to do with Tara. You started the session talking about dark premonitions that you had at the end of that tarot session with the young girl who was kidnapped. Something doesn't ring true here. If you knew something evil was headed her way, then why were you so surprised when the police called?"

I started, "I try not to believe in that superstitious nonsense. Premonitions, bah, humbug. And don't get me started on the police. Cops are nothing but the corporate enforcers of the prison-industrial complex. They—"

She interrupted me, "Warren, I know that you hate the police. Considering your history, that's very understandable. However, that doesn't answer my question. What did you feel when the police called?"

"That wasn't the question you asked," I said.

"It is now."

Rose Janeworth is one of the few people in my life whom I let push me around like this. I was sitting where I always sit, feet propped up on a coffee table, leaning back in a well-upholstered chair, glancing over at Rose and then looking out the window of her therapy room.

Rose saw clients out of her wood-shingled cottage in Kensington, an unincorporated village in the hills just north of Berkeley. The home looked like it was just air-lifted from Nottingham: cobblestone walkways, a wisteria-covered porch, a peaked roof, and a view to die for. The sun had set an hour ago, and I could look across the Bay to San Francisco glittering in the night like a tiara.

I turned my chair so that I was no longer hypnotized by the view. Facing Rose, I smiled. She had caught me at one of my games. I'd started one of my anti-authority tirades as a way of avoiding her question.

Rose didn't fit the picture of therapist, which was one of the reasons I trusted her so much. She was in her seventies or eighties. She had clear, robin's-egg-blue eyes, high cheekbones, deep laugh lines, and a chin and neck that could be an advertisement for the rewards of plastic surgery. She was dressed in a green and orange Citron blouse with the image of a dragon flying across it and a long, sheer, flowing orange skirt. Stylish sandals laced up her calfs. One gorgeous emerald set into a gold necklace completed her ensemble. For an old lady, she was damn good-looking.

I'd been seeing Rose on Wednesday nights for three years, ever since the nightmares came back. She knew from the beginning that I didn't want to tell her about my past. Early on in our therapy she broke the rules. She told me about some of her misdeeds, like how she got that emerald she was wearing. She had guts. By busting herself first she'd made it safe for me to share a few of my misdemeanors.

Rose knew enough about my history to send me away to prison for the rest of my life. But she'd been a bad girl, too. We both had the goods on each other. I trusted her as much as I trusted anyone. Which wasn't all that much.

She'd caught me trying to avoid her question. Now all she had to do was sit still and let me twist around in the silence. She sat there, quiet like a snake, waiting for my move. Finally, I said, "At first, getting into the tarot gig was just a con game for me. I'd read a couple of books to get a feel for it. Then I just told people what they wanted to hear. It took a couple of years before reading the cards started getting to me. Even now it surprises me, the things that come out of my mouth. I say to myself, 'Where the hell did that come from?'" Rose waited for more.

"Yeah, I knew that Heather was about to step into a big pile. But another part of me was still thinking that I was making all this tarot shit up."

Rose said, "And then she was kidnapped. The cop called you, and—" She loved those incomplete sentences, the ones that cranked you open like a crowbar.

"Yeah, Herr Inspector Robert Flatfoot, from the Danville Police Department. He asked me how I knew Heather. I acted stupid until he told me about that card with my name and phone number on it. Then I figured what the hell, we could trade. So I told him a little and then he told me a little and then I told him everything I knew and then he didn't haul my ass into the station."

I turned back to the view. I watched as fog obliterated the Golden Gate Bridge and threatened to smother the whole city.

Rose knew we weren't through with this subject. She let the silence sit there for a while. Then she said, "Something more is bothering you. Spill it."

I didn't want to go to the heart of the matter, so I took a detour. "You know I could have been a cop."

"Really?"

"Yeah, I was a gung-ho American when I was in high school and early college. Daddy was a war hero. I wanted him to be proud of me. I was Mr. "America First." So I did football, and ROTC, and was on the fast track for Vietnam. Expert marksman with both handgun and rifle. I got a leadership award from our ROTC summer camp, which I later burned along with my draft card.

"Mom was a peacenik, a Quaker, and hopelessly naive. I held her in complete contempt, just like Dad did.

"I was shocked when my ROTC officer called me into his

36

office one morning and told me I was no longer a member of the corps. No explanation, except to say that I would be receiving a 4F deferment from my draft board in a few weeks and that I should never attempt to enlist. When I protested, he tossed me out of his office. He was disgusted with me. I had no idea why.

"It took two years before my mother confessed. She'd written my draft board a letter that went something like, 'Dear Sirs: I am thrilled that my son is in ROTC, and I feel certain that he will make a fine officer. He will join a long tradition in my family of brave soldiers. His father was decorated with a purple heart, and I know how much it means for Richard to follow in his footsteps. There is one problem, which may be a little difficult for Richard in the service. He is an active homosexual, usually dating a couple of different men a week. We have taken him to counseling, but nothing seems to help. He just can't keep his hands off other guys. I don't know how you handle this problem in the military, but if I could recommend that he be put into an all-homosexual squad, I'm sure it will work out fine. Thanks for all you are doing in the war effort. Sincerely, Margaret Green.' That did the job," I said.

Rose said, "That's a great story. Got to love those moms! But your history isn't what's bothering you tonight."

I still wanted to stay oblique. I said, "Back at Princeton I was a lit major. I memorized a poem by Matthew Arnold. It ends:

> *'Ah, love, let us be true*
> *To one another! for the world, which seems*
> *To lie before us like a land of dreams,*
> *So various, so beautiful, so new,*
> *Hath really neither joy, nor love, nor light,*
> *Nor certitude, nor peace, nor help for pain;*

And we are here as on a darkling plain
Swept with confused alarms of struggle and flight,
Where ignorant armies clash by night.' "

After a pause, Rose said, "Very eloquent. We're closer. I got that the world is a dangerous place. Now, what's that got to do with how you felt when the policeman called?"

I went on another tangent. That's the way I work in therapy. I go on a detour and Rose finds a way to weave it toward the truth in the center. I said, "I saw a short cartoon once called *Bambi Meets Godzilla*. Bambi is dancing through the woods, and then Godzilla steps on her. That's the whole film."

Rose said, "Heather was Bambi, and you should have warned her about Godzilla."

I got up and walked over to the window. Rose had figured it out, damn her. Looking out at the darkness, I said, "I should have told her something. I saw it coming and all I did was joke about her boyfriend. Maybe if she knew evil was headed right toward her she could have protected herself. But, as usual, I did nothing."

Rose said, "Healthy guilt inspires one to take action. While you're feeling guilty, you might find out how you can help her, or her family. That way you won't waste your guilt on useless attacks of self-hatred. Instead, you can harness that guilty energy and use it to make amends to Heather. We're going to need to end here for tonight. I'll see you next week."

I took one last look out the window. The diamond lights of the city were gone. All I could see across the water was a greenish-yellow pile of fog. It was heading toward me across the bay. Soon the wet, gray nothingness would engulf us, too. Then the stars would go out.

CHAPTER EIGHT

I was down in the belly of an ocean liner. The engine was on fire. I had to get out of there. I kept shoving people out of my way. I was trying to get to the Grand Staircase. I could see it just ahead, the red-carpeted stairs rising to the Promenade Deck. But the crowd got ugly and started pushing me back down.

I opened my eyes and sat up in bed, still half struggling. Damn, another nightmare. I rolled out of bed, took a leak, and put on the water for a pot of Assam tea. It was Friday. No chores today.

My day of rest ended as soon as I took my messages off my voice mail. My sister Tara called my 800 number and left this message:

"I don't want to see you, but I have to. There's stuff about the family you need to know, even though you don't deserve to know anything about any of us, since you lied to us and betrayed us for thirty years.

"I'm stuck in Berkeley for six months on a temporary teaching assignment. I'll keep running into you, so we'd better get this shit out of the way, so I can just ignore you for the rest of my life. I don't know too much about this town, so meet me at the fountain at Sather Gate at ten this morning. Or even better yet, don't show up, and then I can just write you off.

"Oh, and by the way, this meeting is going to be a one-way communication: me talking to you. I don't want to hear some lie about what you've done. There is no excuse for what you did. Good-bye."

I looked at the clock. I had an hour. I took one of the greeting cards that I kept in my desk. It was the image of the Fool from the Rider-Waite tarot deck. A young vagabond was looking up at the sunny sky as he blithely walked off a cliff. His faithful white dog was looking up at his master. Fido's about to go over the edge, too. Inside the card was blank. I wrote Tara a note:

Dear Tara:

I was a fool. I am honoring your request not to explain or defend myself during our meeting. When I was twenty-three, I made the choice to go very far underground, so far that even the underground doesn't know that I'm alive. I would have been killed, or imprisoned for the rest of my life, depending on who got to me first. And there's no statute of limitations on what I did. If they knew I was alive, both the law and some very nasty lawless guys would still want to take my life.

But there hasn't been a day since then that I don't wish I could have made another choice. I'm mentally messed up, manic-depressive and in ongoing therapy, mostly because I've had to live with this lie all my adult life.

I'm sorry for all the suffering I have caused you. You're right, there is no adequate justification for putting my family and friends through that much grief. Thanks for giving me the time today that you are going to give me.

I understand that this is probably my last time together with you. I just want you to know you were a great sister to me, and you deserved a much better brother than the one you got.

If you ever want to contact me, my phone number is 510-654-7323 and my address is Warren Ritter, 1814 Euclid St., Apartment #41, Berkeley, CA 94704. I would love to hear from you again, and I respect your decision to keep your distance.

Love,
Richard

I knew this card wouldn't do the job. Nothing I wrote was going to be able to repair what I had destroyed.

Our meeting place was called Ludwig's Fountain, named after a wonderful, Frisbee-catching German shorthair pointer who waded in it daily from 1960 to 1965. There was nothing joyous about Tara's demeanor as I came walking up. She saw me and started walking down the path toward the stream. I hurried to catch up with her.

We walked in silence for a while. Then she spoke. "Dad died in '75 from a heart attack. He was a centurion biker, in perfect health, and married to a girl eighteen years younger than he was. I'm not going to tell Mom about you, since she sometimes forgets who I am these days. I'm a full professor with a Ph.D. in fish and wildlife biology and currently on loan to the Department of Environmental Science, Policy and Management. I'm happily unmarried. That's about all I want to tell you."

I asked, "Where's Dad buried?"

She said, "You haven't earned the right to have any of your questions answered. I've got to go now."

I said, "I wrote you a note. You can read it or just tear it up. Here." I handed her the card. She looked like I had just handed her a full snotrag, but at least she put it in her briefcase.

She said, "Good-bye, Richard," and started to walk off. Then she stopped and turned back to me. She said, "I don't know whether to tell you this or not. I probably shouldn't. I don't think I'll ever give you any more information besides what I'm about to say. You don't deserve even this. But I want you to know that one of the reasons I took this temporary assignment is so that I could be in the Bay Area when my niece has her first baby." Then she turned away and kept walking.

Niece? She's an aunt? How could that be? Her brother would have to have a child. I was her only sibling. Oh, I must be a father. And it sounded like I was about to become a grandfather. Shit.

CHAPTER NINE

My father was dead. My father was dead, and my mother had the cognitive prowess of a jellyfish. I didn't feel too much right now about my mother. Freud said I loved her, but I don't remember the affair that well. I think it was short-lived on both of our parts. Mostly I remember her annoying me.

But my father was dead. His heart stopped. I had enough experience with Dad's cold heart not to be surprised. There were nights after a good whipping when I'd wondered if he even *had* a heart.

But he was no longer on Earth. Even though it happened years ago, I was just noticing the difference. The sun was bleached today. The car horns sounded muted. Even the air was thinner.

I was doing a late afternoon shift at my table. The tarot cards I worked with were just images on cardstock, randomly distributed and ultimately meaningless. My clients were pretty meaningless, too. Life had drained into the bay, leaving behind husks, shells, rinds, and shards. It was going to be a long weekend.

It was a week since I had given Heather her reading. The story was still front page, but nothing new had happened. Rose had told me to find out how to help Heather's family.

Hell, I had no chance of doing that. I couldn't even deal with my family. My family that had members in it I had never met and members I would never meet again. The family that I had deserted.

There was no way I was going to be able to save little Heather, or not-so-little Heather. I couldn't do much of anything. My father was dead.

I went home and got drunk. It didn't help.

"So, how does it work?" Jim McNally asked.

"People pay me money and I make shit up," I answered.

It was a chilly, damp Sunday morning. Any sane person was at home eating croissants and reading the paper. That left a handful of hungry street vendors, including me, and my cop friend Mac to keep each other company. He was sitting at my table, spreading out the cards to look at them.

"Come on, Warren. Be straight with me. You're reading these weird little cards. You're not looking at people's palms or doing astrology. What do you see when you lay them out?"

"I see a way to make a living and never have to walk into Nordstrom again."

"Stop with the bullshit, okay? I get jive all day. I'm serious. Let's do an experiment. You give yourself a reading. I'll sit behind you. You tell me what you see."

"Pay me?"

"Screw you, you're getting the reading. Do it out of your fear of me."

I said, "Now *that's* a good reason. I quake as I deal the cards."

I didn't mind talking with Mac about this. My hangover was lifting and there was nothing else to do. Besides, I hadn't talked about how I do what I do before. The longer I worked at this, the more I realized that it wasn't a 100 percent con job. There was something about those cards. I lectured as I shuffled the pack.

"Most tarot readers use fancy-dancy layouts like the Celtic Cross. They put tons of significance on where in the spread the card falls. They've got a position for the Higher Self, the Recent Past, Hopes and Fears, Ultimate Outcome, junk like that.

"I'll use position sometimes, especially if I feel that my client expects it. But I'm more intrigued with the energy vectors that flow between the cards than I am about where they fit into some pattern I superimpose on them.

"This is the X spread. Five cards. I just have two positions, below the middle and above the middle. The card in the middle is you right now, or in this case, me right now. It's what hot-shot tarot readers call the Significator in order to sound professional."

I pulled out the Significator card first. "So in this reading—oh, shit, there it is again. I have five cards that haunt me these days. They come up in almost every reading. And one of them is right there, as my Significator, the Hanged Man." On the card a man hung upside down, his ankles strung up over his head. He looked oddly peaceful, considering his position.

"It means one of two things. It can represent mellow hanging out, peaceful waiting, a person not yet ready to make his move. Or it can stand for being strung up, trapped, tied up, and tipped over. In this case it's probably door number two."

I dealt two cards below the Significator. It didn't look good. "The bottom two cards represent the forces in the past or your unconscious that are influencing you. And here's another one of

45

my plague cards: the Tower. Things that I hold as solid in my life are about to crumble. But next to it is a sweet card, the Six of Cups. Two kids are playing in a garden. This card can represent positive memories of childhood."

There's my sister, coming back into my life. I wasn't about to touch that dial with Mac, so I went on, "So two things are welling up in my psyche: childhood memories and the potential collapse of my personality."

I cut the deck and got ready to put two cards on the top of the spread. "The upper loop is about what faces me in my immediate future. It's about what happens when my energy hits the world."

It was one of those days. "Let's see what we've got here. Damn, another plague card, Death. Novice tarot readers freak out when they get the Death card. All by itself, Death usually isn't that big a deal in a spread. It just signifies something dropping away. Of course, it's not all by itself today."

"What's that mean?" Mac asked. Curious bugger.

"Look how they bunch together toward the middle. Death, the Hanged Man, and the Tower, all nearly touching each other. That's a clump of negative energy, and it's all focused down into the Tower. A lot of my life is just about to get stripped away. I'd better look out.

"The other card up here is the Lovers. A couple stands hand in hand with an angel overhead blessing them. This card represents intimacy and relationship."

Mac said, "You're finally going to get laid?"

"That would be nice. So the whole spread is saying my past is going to kick my ass, and I might fall apart, die, stay paralyzed, or fall in love."

"How do you know which outcome will happen?"

"Wrong question," I said. "The right question is, 'What do I need to learn from this situation?' I'll turn over another card to find out. The Ace of Cups. Interesting.

"It's all about my heart. The emotional birth of my heart. My heart is hung upside down. I'm paralyzed right now. Hell is coming my way. If I can keep my heart open, I'll grow. If I close down, I'll die."

I'd always looked forward to dying. It felt like dropping a load of guilt, responsibility, and struggle. But today, face-to-face with a reading as dangerous as Heather's, I realized that I wasn't ready to go.

I might never get to see my daughter. Who was she? Did she have any of her father's fire? Would she want to see me if she knew I existed? Or would she hate me? I had to know.

A big clump of feelings crawled up from my stomach and lodged in my throat. I fought against the threatening wetness in the corners of my eyes.

This was getting way too personal. I needed to lighten things up. I turned to Mac, "Now, does all that gobbledy-goop answer your question?"

He said, "You know, I think it does. I see that it's not about looking definitions up in a book or saying, 'This card in that place means this.' When you're reading you look like you're listening to the cards, learning from them. Very cool. Thanks."

Mac got a call on his walkie-talkie and had to split. I gathered up the cards, relieved to be alone. That reading was too damn real. I kept thinking about the daughter I didn't know and about Heather being held captive. And about the Eight of Swords. Heather and I were connected. Something was being held captive inside me, too. I just didn't know what.

CHAPTER TEN

I was getting ready for another busy, empty day. As I was setting up my table, I noticed a plump woman standing next to the bookstore. She wasn't dressed Berkeley. She wore a navy wool skirt, a beige silk blouse with cute French cuffs, and a paisley scarf fastened with a circle pin inlaid with tiny pearls. Definitely not Berkeley.

The minute she saw my sign, "Tarot Card Readings: Discover Your Destiny!" she came over and asked, "Are you the only tarot reader in Berkeley?"

"Well, the only one on Telegraph Avenue. Why?"

"You don't know me. I am Louise Wellington, the mother of Heather Wellington, the girl who was . . ."

After a pause I said, "Yeah, I know who she is."

She said, "The last time I talked with her she said she was getting a reading. I haven't seen any other tarot readers, so I figured she must have been with you just before . . ."

No wonder she couldn't bring herself to say the word. She was so scared. She had more to say, so I waited.

"Well, the reason I wanted to speak to you . . . I mean . . . I don't know if Heather told you, but I do a bit of tarot and astrology myself. Just as a hobby, you know."

I nodded again. Mr. Enigmatic.

"Well, I was wondering . . . would it be possible to see the spread you did for Heather?"

"Why?"

"Well, they haven't found any clues, and there haven't been any ransom notes, and I . . . I don't know where else to turn."

I shook my head. "I don't know how I can assist you—" I was getting ready to cut her loose. Then I remembered what Rose had said about helping the family. Oh, well, I never got many clients before noon anyway. I could do a little pro bono work. So I ended that sentence, "—but I can show you her reading as best I remember it. My name's Warren Ritter."

I started going through the deck, looking for the right cards. I remembered that spread pretty damn well. The cursed cards kept pursuing me.

I laid out all Heather's cards and included the Death card in the spread this time. When I was finished, I looked up. Louise Wellington's face was ashen. I wondered if she was about to faint.

I got up and opened a chair for her and helped her sit down. Then I walked around and sat on my side of the table. Neither of us spoke for a while.

Louise said, "Oh, my God. This is terrible. Is she dead?"

"How would I know?" I asked.

"You're the psychic. Ask the cards! I need to know!"

I sighed and started to invent a reason why this wouldn't work. "Look, Mrs. Wellington . . ."

"Call me Louise."

For a moment I felt what it must be like to have a daughter

disappear. To come to me, Louise must be grasping at straws. But if straws are all you can find on the surface of the water, reaching out for them sure beats drowning in despair. I knew fear that comes when you are standing on the edge of hopelessness. I decided to help her.

I said, "I can't tell you if she's alive or not. But here's what I can do. I'll do a five-card reading. It doesn't mean anything, but maybe we'll learn something from it. No charge. Let's just see what the cards say." I took out one card and then began shuffling the deck.

"I am going to take the Eight of Swords and place it in the center of the spread. That is the Significator, representing Heather where she is right now. Then I'll place four cards around her, representing her internal resources, her external resources, her adversaries, and the probable outcome in the next week or so."

I dealt them out. "So what do we have here? For her internal resources we got the Seven of Wands. Here the courageous warrior is fighting adversity with valor and persistence. Does this seem like Heather?"

"Oh, yes!" Louise said. "She's unafraid. That's led to all sorts of conflicts with her teachers and with my current husband, but she had—I mean she *has* a lot of courage." She smiled at me, although the worry lines on her brow remained tight. That smile was so reminiscent of Heather's smile. She admired her daughter's feistiness.

I said, "Good. She'll need it. Next, the card representing exterior resources is the Magician. Somewhere in the universe there is a man with creative intelligence, power, and skill. This guy, maybe with dark hair, is on her side. Could that be your husband?" I looked up at her. She shook her head but said nothing. I tried again, "Or some boyfriend?" Another headshake. "Or maybe it's someone we don't know about yet. But someone with vision and discipline is working for her release.

"Her adversary is represented by the King of Swords. This is someone who is fiercely emotional and very intelligent, determined, ruthless, maybe with dark hair and gray eyes. The good news is that he is smart. He might be willing to negotiate Heather's release to get what he wants." Her smile disappeared the minute I said the word "ruthless" and I don't think she heard anything after that.

She asked, "Is there anything there about a black man. Her new boyfriend is from Oakland, and I don't trust him a bit."

I said, "No, nothing in this reading that points to race. However, look, finally here is some good news. The card for the immediate future is Judgment. The dead are rising from their graves to be reborn. It represents setting free what has been entombed or imprisoned. Looking at these cards, it seems that she might still be alive."

Louise's shoulders dropped an inch. She said, "Thank God! I so hope you're right. This is the first deep breath I've taken in a week. Thank you so much for this reading. It really helps me keep hoping."

I was grateful that I had lightened her burden. Then, like a dope, I had to add one more thing. I put my label on the Eight of Swords and handed it to her. "Here's my card. Let me know if there is any way I can help you or your family. I don't know what I can do, but call me if you need to."

She thanked me again. Okay, enough was enough! She got up to go. I started collecting my cards to put them back in their black silk drawstring bag.

One card dropped out and landed on the sidewalk. Whenever a card falls out unexpectedly, I take it as a sign. I believe the card came out to tell us something more about the reading. I almost called Louise back until I looked down and saw which card lay on the sidewalk.

It didn't matter that New Age readers insist that this card signifies profound transformative change. As Freud said, when someone asked him what a cigar symbolized in his dream, "Sometimes a cigar is just a cigar." Sometimes things mean just what they say. I picked up the Death card and tucked it back into the pack. She was the mother of a daughter in danger. Louise didn't need this piece of feedback.

Late that Sunday evening, the phone rang. Once, weekends had been an open invitation to let out the party animal inside me. I'd prowl the streets till dawn, looking for action. Those nights were long gone. That evening found me asleep in my chair, a book open on my lap.

It took me a second to reorient from the dream mansion that I was trapped in to my living room. I finally found the phone and answered it, "Ritter."

Louise was whispering to me on the phone. "You were right, she's alive! We got a call. There's a letter coming from her. They want a million dollars. I think we're going to get her back soon! I'm so relieved. I knew you'd want to know. I just wanted to let you know she's okay. Frank doesn't like me talking to psychics, so I've got to go, but thank you so much."

She hung up before I got to say a word.

CHAPTER ELEVEN

People live. People die. People get kidnapped. People disappear. People get blown up. None of it's my affair. I wanted to be done with Louise, Heather, and all the rest. Story over. Eventually, I might have forgotten the whole incident, if someone hadn't tried to frame me for murder.

It was 8:00 Monday morning. I'd finished my chores. I headed for Caffé Mediterraneum. I had to hike across the campus, but it was worth it. Rigid personalities need their lattes perfect. The Med had been there since eggheads, hipsters, and beatniks foraged along the Ave. New owners tried to turn it into an art gallery and jazz club, but this early in the morning its true nature was apparent: caffeine's version of an opium den. Later in the day, leathered, punctured teenagers would hang out in front to scare the tourists away. But this early, it was just wasted students and untenured professors who frequented the joint. It was a serious crowd. We came there to fix up on caffeine, and it had all the warmth of a crack house.

This place suited me. No one welcomed me by name or gave

a shit about how I was on this lovely day. The Iranian behind the counter slammed down my daily dose, a triple nonfat latte, and turned away. I sat in my usual seat by the window, opened my *Chronicle*, and watched coeds on their way to class, adjusting their panty hose. A few things have gotten better since the sixties, and one of them is the way women students dress.

The latte was steaming on the table in front of me. I was waiting for the glass to cool before I started creating white mustaches. I shook open the paper and got ready to immerse myself in the mind-numbing drivel that passes for journalism in this country.

Wham, my day went to shit.

TRAGEDY STRIKES TWICE IN DANVILLE
Robert Martinez, Chronicle Staff Writer

Frank Wellington has had his life torn apart. Last week his daughter was kidnapped. An eyewitness in Berkeley reported her getting pulled into a van. Her backpack showed up in Oakland. But other than that, police could uncover no evidence of her whereabouts. It took a week before a ransom demand arrived. This weekend a call finally came. The kidnappers asked for $1 million in ransom money. Then Sunday night Mrs. Wellington disappeared.

In a short statement to the media, Mr. Wellington stated, "I have no idea what has happened to the two most precious people in my life. If the kidnappers have my wife, too, please contact me. I don't know what to do!"

Mr. Wellington gave a longer phone interview to this writer late last night. He said that his wife had been getting more and more desperate over the week. He overheard her talking to a psychic on the phone, and soon afterward she got in her car and drove off. She said nothing to him about where she was going. That was the last he's heard from her.

Danville Police Detective Robert Flemish released the following statement, "Mr. Wellington contacted the station Sunday evening reporting the disappearance of his wife. Because of the disappearance of their daughter, we immediately began a missing person's investigation. Upon Mr. Wellington's request, the Federal Bureau of Investigation is joining local police in the hunt for the missing Wellington women."

Turn to TRAGEDY: Page A-11 Col. 1

I tossed the paper on the table and took a searing swig of my latte. I was in deep trouble. Phone records would identify the "psychic" she had talked to. Here I was again, the last person to talk with one of the Wellingtons who "disappeared." I considered my options.

Option one: I could fade away. "Warren Ritter" was only one of three well-established identities that I used. I could sell my hybrid Civic, get on my bike, and head north to Spokane, Washington, to become "David Ellbruck." Or I could even go farther, to Alaska, and move into my deep cover, my "Raymond Defresco" persona.

But I liked Berkeley. It was a great fit for me. And I'd done a lot of work to build the background for my Ritter identity. I hated to throw all that work away. Plus, I didn't want anyone, including the police, to think I was a kidnapper.

That left Option two: Tough it out. So far as I knew, my fingerprints weren't on record anywhere. Warren Ritter maintained his residence in Nevada. All my identities had driver's licenses from states where you didn't get fingerprinted or photographed. I'd always wondered if this ID could endure an FBI check. I knew that I was about to find out.

I would have to be Mr. Good Citizen and help my local police state. I pulled out my cell phone, checked the number given in the article, and connected with the Danville Police Department. I asked to speak to Robert Flemish, trying not to put too much emphasis on the "phlegm." Damn, he was in.

"Hello, Bobby," I began (I can't stop myself from trying to offend these guys). "It's Warren Ritter, Berkeley's top tarot reader."

"Yeah," he said. He must have learned that minimal response trick too.

"Well, I was reading the paper this morning, and I found that article about Mrs. Wellington's disappearance. I saw your name and thought I should talk with you. She came to talk to me in Berkeley yesterday and called me last night. I wanted to talk with someone involved with the investigation to see if I could help out in any way."

How was that for earning a Boy Scout merit badge for good citizenship?

Flemish said, "I do have some questions for you. I'd like you to come in. What's your schedule?"

"Actually, Officer Flemish, I'm calling from my cell phone. I'm on the way to do a reading for a private client right now. Is it possible to do this by phone?" See, I was trying to be nice. Lying, but still trying.

He said, "I can ask you some preliminary questions but I may need to see you in person later. Other investigators may also need to speak with you."

I said, "Yes, I heard the FBI is being brought in. Too bad. I think they'll probably just screw things up and get in your way.

You local police know the territory a hell of a lot better than some out-of-town fed. But I'll cooperate any way I can."

Flemish started to speak, "I'm glad to hear that, Mr. Ritter—"

I interrupted him, "You can call me Warren, Officer." Butter wouldn't melt in my mouth.

"It's not 'Officer,' it's 'Detective Flemish,' but you can call me Robert." Oh ho, a little familiarity here. Maybe dissing the FBI won me some credit.

"Thank you, Robert. Let me tell you about the two conversations I had with Mrs. Wellington, and then you can ask me whatever questions you have."

My new friend agreed, and I told him everything I could remember about the meeting with Louise and the late-night phone call. He was curious about what she had said about the ransom note and whether she had said anything about leaving the house. Which of course she hadn't.

No one could alibi me for the time before or after Louise's call. But Detective Phlegm didn't sound too suspicious. After all, I had reached out. We ended our conversation quite amicably. I'd made my second good impression with this guy. I think it was that crack I made about the feds. Local police hate FBI agents almost as much as they hate criminals. The enemy of my enemy is my friend.

CHAPTER TWELVE

After getting back to the apartment, I did the most onerous task of the day—I logged on to my e-mail. Whatever happened to the days when folks wrote letters that took days to get to you? Then you could take days crafting a reply. And everybody enjoyed the process. Now it's instant reply, hurry up, and folks get pissed if you take twelve hours to reply to their urgent message.

I may be a troglodyte, but I'm a canny troglodyte. Just because I hate the Internet was no reason not to work it. I had my own tarot Web site, and I did e-mail readings on a regular basis for busy or distant clients. But I avoided my computer like the plague on weekends. I work too hard during those days to work Saturday and Sunday evenings, too.

The best time to clear my mailbox was just after my morning caffeine fix. So I logged on around 10 o'clock to troll for clients. There were two new e-mails, both from LouiseWell@ hotmail.com.

The first one was sweet, but knowing what I knew now, it was also a bit eerie: "Dear Warren: Thank you so much for your help today. I had to get off the phone quickly just now. I didn't have time to tell you how much I appreciated you setting my mind at ease earlier today. Frank, my husband, is a dear man and a devoted father to Heather. He even adopted her, which he didn't need to do. But he has his opinions, and unfortunately he doesn't share our fascination with the higher realms. You are very talented, and I hope you go far in your career. Not only are you an excellent psychic, but also you are very kind. Again thank you for all your support. Louise."

I opened the second one and read, "Dear Warren: Come to the bench in the park by the creek at the end of 8th Street at 12 noon today. I have something I need to show you. I'm willing to pay for your time. Please! Louise Wellington."

I was surprised that she even knew about that pocket park. I didn't want her money. But there was a note of desperation in her e-mail. I deleted my messages and got ready to go meet her.

When people think of Berkeley, they think of the university, with its green lawns and spacious libraries. Or perhaps they picture Telegraph Avenue: the head shops, used clothing stores, and street vendors making it look irretrievably stuck in the 1960s. They sure don't think about Eighth Street.

The Berkeley flats are made up of working-class neighborhoods squeezed between industrial districts. The run-down houses are becoming gentrified as house prices soar. Soccer fields are going in, and esoteric outlet stores are trying to upscale the slums. But Eighth Street is still a rough place to hang out after dark. Going north on it you head into the heart of an ugly industrial area filled with old warehouses, zinc-plating factories, auto muffler repair shops, and weed-encrusted empty lots enclosed by rusty chain-link fences.

From a block away it looks like the north end of Eighth Street wanders off into University Village. This is a housing complex for the underpaid teaching assistants and graduate students who do most of the face-to-face teaching at the university. But when you illegally park in the Employees Only lot and walk farther north, you find yourself in a tiny park that meanders along the edge of Cordonices Creek.

All of a sudden the ugliness disappears. You can sit on a rustic bench and listen to the whisper of water over rocks, accompanied by the arias of songbirds. For a sanguine moment you can forget the global pollution that is going on just down the street. This park is known by the locals as the Secret Path. The United States Postal Service paved the loveliest part of it to put in a parking lot for their Package Transfer Station. But a tiny northern leg still exists. Its existence is a well-guarded secret.

I saw a University Police car in the Employees Only lot, so I decided to head for the north end of the trailhead. Tenth Street dead-ends at a fence. Only the most observant person would notice a tiny sign on the left marking the beginning of the path. But this street was occupied today. A man was sitting in his ebony Beemer, talking excitedly into a cell phone. I imagined he was a real estate agent and his escrow was falling apart. Bye-bye $7,000 commission. No other cars there. Where had Louise parked? Maybe she was running late.

I made a U-turn and drove away. Something didn't feel quite right about all this. For some reason I didn't want Mr. Top Agent of the Month to see me wandering around. My survival instincts had served me well during the past thirty years. When I start feeling itchy, I always follow that itch. Better to be a little late than to be busted.

I knew a concealed entrance to Secret Path Park that would allow me to get to the bench unseen by Mr. Coldwell Banker. I parked in the reserved lot for the agents of Wilderness Travel, hidden behind a warehouse at the end of Ninth. I walked over to a break in the trees and scrambled down the bank. I had to jump from concrete block to concrete block to get across the stream. Then up the hill and I was on an overgrown path that headed down toward the bench.

Coming from upstream it was easier to see that someone had fallen asleep on the ground in front of the bench. As I got closer I saw that this person was a brunette in a long skirt, not the usual type to be snoozing on the ground. The closer I got, the more it looked like Louise. She was totally still, no sign of movement.

I stopped a few feet away, hands in my pockets, breathing shallowly. I stared at a fly that had discovered this new treat. It was circumnavigating the small round hole in her left temple. Around the black entrance there was a star-shaped pattern of tiny red marks.

I stood motionless and looked around. I could see the employee parking lot, but no one from the street could have seen Louise's crumpled body. No cars came by. I knew that every movement I made could leave trace evidence that could convict me. She had been dumped in front of the bench and her purse tossed on top of her body. Some of the contents had spilled out of the purse, and her cell phone had tumbled onto the path. It lay at my feet. I picked it up and put it in my pocket. I thought I might be able to check out whom she called last and find out who killed her.

Then I realized that I was in deep doo-doo. I had to get out of there. I began backing away from the corpse, smudging my footprints in the dirt as I retraced my steps. These shoes would have to be destroyed.

I got back to the place on the bank where I had crossed the stream. This time I tripped and stepped ankle deep into the water. I didn't really care. I scrambled up the steep embankment. The earth was disturbed. It wouldn't take the police long to find where I had crawled up. I stood at the top and looked around. No one in sight.

I walked calmly over to my car and sat sidewise on the driver's seat, my feet still on the concrete. With a piece of stiff cardboard I carefully scraped off the mud that had deposited itself on the soles of my wet shoes. I moved slowly, making sure none of the dirt got into my car.

After my shoes were cleaner, I took them and my socks off. I wiped down the shoes, hoping to remove any fingerprints and hair. I walked around to the trunk in my bare feet. I put the cardboard, the shoes, and my soggy socks in a plastic bag. I would toss my socks in the laundry as soon as I got home. The shoes were a goner. Luckily, I had a pair of Birkenstocks in the trunk. I put them on and drove away.

I went to the parking lot of a nearby Taco Bell, parked in the shade, and turned on the car radio. I checked Louise's cell phone, but the last number dialed was my apartment. That was no help. Then I just sat and waited to hear what I knew would be coming soon. First I heard the sirens. It didn't take long for the all-news station to pick it up.

The perky voice of the announcer said, "There's a late-breaking story from Berkeley. Dawn Lester has the report. Dawn?"

A more sultry voice began, "We've just received word that

the body of a woman has been discovered in a park in Berkeley. We have no more details available at this time, but we expect more information on the identity of the body momentarily."

I turned off the radio and started to drive. I wandered around until I found a street that was lined with gray garbage cans. In Berkeley, homeowners hauled these wheeled containers to the curb on trash-collection day.

I stopped and looked around. I was alone. I opened the lid of one of the wheeled Dumpsters, to make sure the garbage hadn't been picked up yet. It was three-quarters full. I dropped my shoes into it. Damn, those were alligator-skin loafers. Au revoir.

Then I went home and crawled into bed. I wanted to throw up. I just lay there for hours, shivering, trying not to think, trying not to remember.

I don't have a TV. So every evening that I'm not working on the Ave, I turn my radio to the all-news station at 6:00 P.M. I listen for about fifteen minutes until I get good and mad at popular media and how it has gagged itself on the corporate right-wing view of the world. Then I turn over to KPFA evening news and listen to the more realistic left-wing spin on things. Tonight I knew what the lead story was going to be:

"What began as a disappearance and turned into a kidnapping has now become a murder, and the whereabouts of the young girl, Heather Wellington, is *still* unknown. Our reporter in Berkeley, Dawn Lester, has been following this story since a body was discovered at noon today in Berkeley. Dawn?"

"Last weekend, Heather Wellington, a teenager from Danville, was apparently abducted in the middle of the day on a busy street in downtown Berkeley. Then, last Sunday night, her mother, Mrs. Louise Wellington, also disappeared.

"There was no word of Louise Wellington's whereabouts

until noon today, when the police received an anonymous tip. Her body was discovered lying behind a park bench in a secluded park in the flats of Berkeley.

"She had been shot in the head. Berkeley Police Detective Marvin Stiller had this to say about today's disturbing discoveries . . ." I turned it off. I didn't want to hear another cop.

Someone wanted me there when the cops showed up. Someone was staking out that murder scene and spotted me going down that path. Someone who had my e-mail address. Someone who probably murdered Louise.

I stay away from quests for justice. In my youth, those quests got me in a lot of trouble. These days, I just read my cards and keep focused on simple survival. I try to avoid looking around too intently. I take no action to alleviate the sins of my society: racism, spousal and child abuse, international economic exploitation, ecological rape, and Americans' deeply held hatred for anything that's not the white, patriarchal, straight, middle-class norm. Violence is the Amerikan way, and nothing I can do will change it.

But this murder was different. It happened on my turf. And somebody sent me those e-mails. Somebody wanted me on the spot when the net closed. Someone was trying to hang this thing on me.

You know, maybe if I hadn't just found out that I was a father I would have shit-canned the whole thing and taken off. But somehow Heather and my daughter and Louise's fierce desire to protect her baby got all mixed together in my heart. By the time the reporter was finished with her report, a beast deep inside me crawled out of its den. Kids aren't supposed to get kidnapped. Moms aren't supposed to get killed. At least not on my watch. I was going to make this motherfucker pay!

CHAPTER THIRTEEN

It was time to marshal some troops. I spent much of the night thinking and taking notes. I slept fitfully. Once an hour or so, my eyes would open wide, and I'd roll over and jot something else down on my action list.

Tuesday morning I woke up hard. Paranoid alertness wrestled with utter exhaustion. Alertness barely won. I lay in the morning sun, listening to the bells in the Campanile. My body ached for more sleep and my mind raced with all the things I needed to do.

To outdo the police, I needed three things: money, information, and manpower. Money was no problem. One of the false identities I created, David Ellbruck from Spokane, had taken a small nest egg fifteen years ago and parlayed it into a comfortable fortune. He bought a lot of stock in a guy named Gates's young, powerhouse software company based in Redmond, Washington.

Dave Ellbruck sent regular consultation payments to his favorite tarot reader, Warren Ritter. Money from myself to myself, all aboveboard, well documented, with income tax gladly paid twice on it.

Rose had asked me once, "If you're so well off, why do you work at places like Nordstrom and Telegraph Avenue?" I told her how the IRS almost busted one of my identities for tax evasion. "Luther Turner" had to die intestate in an auto accident before the feds gave up on the hunt. After that I learned that every identity needed its own income stream. Dave Ellbruck lived off his investments. Warren Ritter had to work part-time.

I had $25,000 in currency stashed away in a storage locker in Antioch. I'd use it to hire personnel. Any necessary future funding would be covered by another check from Mr. Ellbruck.

What I needed right now was information. I'd met a damn good-looking computer expert who was fascinated with the tarot. She'd talked about how a spread of cards could reflect patterns of unfolding processes that were also reflected in current events, relationships, stock market prices, and software trends. It was all about chaos theory, sensitive dependence on initial conditions and synchronicity.

I never understood a word she was saying. But I did her readings and was proud to call her my friend. Sally McLaughlin was an ace hacker. I don't mean hacker in the debased sense of the word: some geeky, overintellectual, socially incompetent computer enthusiast. I mean hacker in the old school way, an outlaw who liked to fuck with security systems. It was time to pay Sally a little visit.

I ignored cleaning the bathroom, grabbed a latte to go, and got into my car. After driving around until I was sure I wasn't being tailed, I headed into a clean, well-lighted neighborhood just outside Berkeley.

I parked three blocks away from my destination and strolled

around. No one was watching me. I finally turned right on Dollard Street and stopped at a blue stucco one-story house. I let
myself through a waist-high gate in the freshly painted white
picket fence. The front yard was a garden with tiny hills, valleys,
and pebbled paths. It had statues of gnomes frolicking around in
it. Such kitsch! Sally told me they did a great job of disguising
her video cameras and motion detectors.

I climbed the stairs next to the ramp that ran up to the front
porch. At the door I nodded toward the camera above me and
pushed the buzzer. I heard a low animal growl and then a
woman's voice saying "Halt, Ripley." Then I heard an electronic
buzz and the sound of the bolt sliding open. I walked in.

The house was built on the floor plan reminiscent of railway
cars. Each room opened in an archway to the one behind it. The
only doors in the house were the front and back ones. They
were made of wood-simulated fiberglass over steel cores. As I
knew from previous visits, even the bathroom had just a curtain
to screen it off. Sally McLaughlin sat on her titanium racing
wheelchair in what would have been the dining room.

Sally had the friendliest face of anyone I'd ever met. She was
always smiling. It was one of those genuine smiles that made
you want to smile back, regardless of how much you'd had to
drink the night before.

She had short, spiky, chocolate-brown hair with thick blond
streaks, glittering chestnut eyes, very broad shoulders, and muscled arms. She played forward on her wheelchair basketball
team, the Wheels of Fortune. It dominated the Berkeley Hoops
League and almost won the state championship last year. She
looked friendly and harmless, and was the most dangerous
woman I knew.

She'd been training to be an army medic when her tenth

thoracic vertebra had been crushed. A jeep ran over her while she was sleeping in the hills behind Fort Dix during a three-day basic training exercise. The government gave her a lifelong pension and then forgot about her. But she didn't forget about them.

I asked her once how she could be cheerful all the time when she had been so fucked over by the army. She giggled and said, "Look, only victims stay resentful. Life is too precious to waste in bitterness and regret. Instead I took my revenge out on the bastards."

She'd developed two obsessions: programming and vengeance. She repeatedly emptied the bank accounts of the soldier who had driven over her sleeping body. The commanding officer, who had swept the accident under the rug, was busted out of the service for collecting child pornography on his computer. He swore he knew nothing about those pictures.

Then Sally went on to bigger and more interesting venues. She succeeded in putting a nuclear missile silo on yellow alert. She released the story of how easy it was to infiltrate our nuclear arsenal to a *New York Times* reporter, pretending to be a concerned male computer operator in the National Security Agency. That began a series of articles in the *Times* about the vulnerability of our nuclear arsenal and a series of forced resignations in the NSA.

She hacked the U.S. embassy database in Tel Aviv and then threatened to expose a list of CIA operatives to Al-Jazeera, unless the United States recognized the Palestine state as more than a bunch of terrorists. She left obscene notes in sensitive files of Bush's reelection committee. She diverted a substantial donation from the National Right to Life Committee to Planned Parenthood. And, as a hobby, she hacked most local Northern California law enforcement computers.

"Hey, Ritter, what the hell are you doing here without warning? Unexpected visitors get greeted by Ripley."

I heard a faint "Rurrr!" to my right and turned to welcome the hundred-pound rottweiler who was alertly sizing me up. The dog's flanks trembled and her lips curled up to reveal long canine incisors.

"Hi, Ripley." I smiled in a very friendly, nonthreatening manner. Ripley was unimpressed. Then I asked Sally, "Come on, release her, please."

"*Vrij,*" Sally said. Ripley came bounding over to lick my face and almost knocked me over. I knew that Sally could just have well said, "*Stellen!*" and Ripley would have leaped for my neck. I liked the friendly greeting better.

Ripley provided a distraction for visitors. Sally needed that in her line of work. Sally could strike three keys while the Tac Squad was dealing with her dog, and all information in her huge database would be completely randomized and then electronically shredded.

Sally's information-gathering services were available for hire for an exorbitant price, but only to a select clientele. Her clients had to agree with her politics, they had to be seeking an end that she approved of, and they had to be extremely discreet.

I'd done five tarot readings for her in this house. We'd become friends. But I'd never contracted for her services before. I was taking our relationship into new territory, and I knew it. But I needed her badly.

After removing Ripley's paws from around my hips, I took the only other chair available in her "office." It was a wire-framed contraption that seemed to shape itself around my spine.

Behind me, lying on their sides, were two eight-foot-long RLX power towers filled with RLX server blades. Her setup was almost as powerful as a room full of supercomputers.

Sally said, "Well, what's up?"

"I didn't call first because I don't know if my line is secure. I need to hire you to do some work for me. Here's the situation . . ."

I told her everything I knew about the kidnapping and the murder. I also let her know that, if this case didn't get solved in a hurry, I was going to have to disappear from the Bay Area. She didn't like a mother getting killed trying to find her daughter. She sure didn't want me to be set up to take the rap for it. I told her what I needed.

"Okay, I can do some of that," she said. "The Danville Police database is no problem. I hacked that three years ago. They set up a brand-new database with holes so big you could drive a Mack truck through it. Within a week they realized their mistake and plugged up those holes. But by then it was too late. I was already recognized by the computer as a systems administrator. Any security programs they add on automatically recognize me and give me access to any information in the system.

"It will cost you two thousand dollars for the current case files on Heather and Louise and one thousand a week for updates. The Berkeley Police mainframe is also a cinch, but it's not worth your time. They still use paper for most of their casework, and the only thing you'll find in that database is payroll records.

"The FBI database is off-limits. I hate to say it, but they have someone better than me working for them. I can't get in there without getting backtracked. It's dangerous even to try these days. Antiterrorism and all that crap."

"Ah, yes, safeguarding us from ourselves. Although in your case that's probably a good idea." I put thirty C-notes wrapped in a rubber band on her desk. "This covers the first two weeks' worth of information."

"Oh, by the way, did you save the e-mails from Louise?" she asked.

"No. I deleted them, and my computer cleans the cache every night. I'm a jerk."

God, she looked cute. Her eyes sparkled. "Hey, Warren, lighten up. Your e-mail password is still 'homesick,' isn't it?"

That didn't feel good. She was everywhere. "Yes," I said shortly. I was changing it tonight.

She saw I was pissed. "Easy, big fella. Don't worry, I keep everything very close to my chest. Maybe the next time you're online I can go inside and see if I can find any trace of the e-mail."

I didn't want her messing around inside my computer any more than she already had. "Never mind. What else do you need?"

She started going through her wide middle desk drawer. I watched her dig deeper into the chaos. She was wiry, intense, and glowing with life. I was damn glad to have her on my side. Eventually she found what she was looking for.

She handed me a small key. "Now, this key opens box thirty-one at Northside Postal Services on Euclid. Any packages in that box will be for you. Put the key back in the box when you're finished using my services. My first delivery should be there tomorrow. Give me your wallet."

Whatever she wanted. After all, she had the dog. I handed my wallet over to her. She opened a box on her desk and removed a small red envelope. Then she took one of her business cards and wrote something on the back of it, and sealed it in the envelope. She put the envelope in my wallet. Handing my wallet back to me she said, "Forget this is in here unless I tell you different. Please don't open it. I'm hoping you will give it back to me at the end of this joyride, still sealed."

"A-OK," I said.

"Now, Warren, I'm in the middle of a big project right now. I don't have time to chat. It's a pleasure doing business with you, and get the hell out of here." She was still smiling.

I took a breath. I had to trust her. I said, "I'll take just one more minute of your time. I have three other questions. One, I need several people tailed by excellent operatives. There may be police tailing the same people. I need my guys to remain undetected by all the other players. Territory may include the Bay Area and Contra Costa County. Who do you recommend?"

Sally said, "I have just the man: Mad Max Valdez. He moved up here from L.A. about a decade ago. His company is Valdez Systems, in Oakland. You can hire muscle from him, bodyguards, armed chauffeurs, security guards, or private investigators. I don't want to know what else you might be able to hire from him.

"But the best thing he has going is his surveillance services. They're among the three best in the Bay Area. One day he told me, 'Hey, nobody notices you if you've got brown skin. Being invisible must be good for something!' "

She reached for a pad of sticky notes, wrote on the top one, ripped it off, and handed it to me. "Here's his address and number. Mention my name, otherwise you might not get in to see him. I'll let him know you are coming. He's not a big fan of gringos, but he likes money, and he likes me."

"Thanks, Sally. The second thing I need, ASAP, is three pieces of information. I need the address and phone number of Heather Wellington's father, Frank. He lives in Danville. And her boyfriend, too, if you can get it. Heather said his first name was Curtis. He's black, and Louise told me he lived in Oakland. Also her ex-boyfriend, name of Hal, who lives in Concord and drives a new silver Grand Am."

"Hey, if she's called them anytime in the last month I'll track them down. Anything else?"

"If you could leave any information you dig up on these guys on my voice mail, I'd appreciate it. Do you want my number?"

"No need. I already have your cell, home, eight hundred, and message service numbers. Which one do you want me to use?"

She was good. No one knew about that message service. It was for very private calls. I said, "Use the cell phone. Okay, now the third thing. I need you to keep an eye out for any sign that I may be a suspect, and especially stay alert for any warrant for my arrest or search warrant for my apartment."

Sally said, "As far as the police go, I'll be able to track Danville but not Berkeley or the feds. This warrant business is harder. A lot of times a judge signs a typed-up warrant. It takes a while for that information to get into the databases. I'll do my best."

"Thanks for everything. I owe you!"

"Oh, don't worry," she said, beaming even brighter, "I'll find new and exciting ways to make you pay. Next time, though, call first from a public booth before dropping in. There are times when I won't answer the door no matter who's on the other side of it. If you had come ten minutes later you'd still be outside. Definitely don't come around for the next twelve hours. I am thawing nasty ice, and once I start I can't stop."

I thanked her, gave Ripley one last cautious pat, and headed for Oakland.

CHAPTER FOURTEEN

Berkeley is surrounded by an irrational maze of one-way streets. I was negotiating my way through it while fishing in my overstuffed glove compartment for my cell phone. Someone yelled, "Watch it, asshole!" I looked up and saw that I'd almost driven into an elderly woman pushing a cart filled with her groceries. She gave me the finger. I deserved it. I yelled out the window, "I'm a jerk! Sorry I scared you. My fault entirely!" She nodded. I hate it when I'm wrong.

Then I pulled over in order to devote my entire attention to the excavation. Finally I unearthed the little critter.

I hate all electronic toys: cell phones, e-mail, PalmPilots, handheld Global Positioning System equipment, and the whole raft of gadgets that intrude on solitude.

When I was a kid I used to disappear into the woods all day. Now I can walk in the wilderness without wasting my valuable time. As I hike along I can call anyone in the world, schedule an appointment, take a picture of me standing next to a tree and then send the person a map so he or she can join me there. Solitude has been snuffed out. I detest these gizmos.

I can't stand them but I use them. I knew that for the duration of this adventure, I'd have to carry the dreaded cell phone around with me. One good reason never to get involved with other people's problems.

A woman's voice answered on the first ring. "Valdez Systems. How may I help you?"

"I'd like to speak to Max Valdez," I said. I heard a click on the other end.

Her voice was warm and friendly. "May I tell him who's calling?"

I'm cautious about giving out my name, any of my names, to strangers, so I said, "I'm a friend of—"

A deep male voice interrupted me, "Please do not speak her name. Did you just leave her house?"

This must be Max. I said, "Yes."

"I just read her e-mail. Come to the office and I'll see you. Good-bye."

Another click and the line went dead. This was an interesting approach to customer service. Well, at least Sally hadn't wasted any time. It looked like my way was paved.

The address was in Fruitvale, a sprawling barrio next to the freeway in West Oakland. There was no sign on the front of any buildings in the area that announced Valdez Security Systems.

I didn't know what to do next. I walked into the Jingletown Grocery and Taqueria and spoke to the back of a man who was hacking away at something on a long wooden counter, "Is there a Valdez Systems building around here?"

He kept chopping. I tried, *"¿Habla inglés?"* the sum total of my non–Taco Bell-based Spanish. The gruff chef turned around and said with a thick accent, "Across the street, the brick building with the blue door." He turned back and continued chopping meat.

Valdez Systems was housed in a converted brick warehouse. Several lines of bolts in the exterior wall attested to the expensive retrofit that made it earthquakeproof. I had missed the small brass plaque next to the entrance with "Valdez Systems" engraved on it. The blue door opened on a reception area done in industrial modern—all brick, chrome, and leather. Behind an aquamarine-tinted glass desk, a stout, attractive brown-skinned woman welcomed me. It was that same hospitable voice I'd heard on the phone.

"I called just a while ago, I'm here to see Max Valdez."

"Of course, Mr. Ritter. My name's Isabel. Welcome. Go up the stairs behind me. Mr. Valdez's office is the door on the left."

I hadn't told her, or Max, my name. Sally must have. I didn't like that. As I climbed the open circular staircase, I worried about what else they might know. At the upper landing were two doors, both painted blue but with no lettering on them, one at each end of the hallway. Turning left, I opened the door to Max Valdez's office.

Max's office was a vast, light space, extending forty feet high to the open roof beams of the warehouse. Windows covered the east and south walls, set into white brick walls. The floors were a blond hardwood, which glistened in the sunlight. There was no desk, just three oversized beige leather executive swivel chairs around a chrome and glass table. A beautiful carved oak armoire stood against one wall, and a large Persian carpet defined the sitting area.

A short, brown bullet of a man met me at the door. He was hard muscled, bald, with thick creases in his face. "I'm Max. Come over here and sit down. Our mutual friend told me about your problem in her e-mail. I want to hear about it from you."

As I walked over to the chairs, I looked out the windows. In the distance the Berkeley-Oakland hills were turning from spring olive to summer tan, but they still looked lovely against an azure blue sky. In those hills, million-dollar mansions looked out over the bay. After a hard day's work on the phone, bosses, owners, CEOs, and top managers of some of the world's largest corporations sat on their glassed-in decks, sipped their single-malt scotches, relaxed from their capitalistic pursuits, and watched the sun set over San Francisco.

Between that hillside Eden and this building stretched the city of Oakland, avaricious, industrialized, impoverished, and menacing. I looked out over deserted factories, abandoned warehouses, Victorians in disrepair, where immigrant families without green cards crammed into two-room slum apartments and English was never spoken.

This was the valley of the disenfranchised: low-level wage earners who had little prospect of ever leaving the few city blocks that bounded their world. Oakland would use them up and then let them rot.

Once I sat down, the walls cut off the lower part of the view. All that remained was the bright, beautiful, distant hills.

I settled into the beige leather, my lumbar supported by a piece of furniture that must have cost a grand. Max sat down across from me, leaned forward, and waited. His brown eyes didn't blink. We were sizing each other up.

Max was wearing a black silk crepe de chine dress shirt with a red Rafaello tie, black wool slacks, and Gucci strap-over slip-ons. The guy had style and the money to indulge it. He also had a look of controlled violence that made me not want to keep him waiting.

Since he was going to be on my team, I told him what I knew about the kidnapping and the murder. He listened, expressionless. This guy was good. When I finished, he said, "And you want what?" His bedside manner was abrupt.

I leaned forward. "Surveillance on the main players as they emerge from this investigation. Your people will have to avoid being spotted by both the suspects and by the police. At this point I see putting a team on the husband and the ex-boyfriend, but others may come out of the woodwork as time goes on."

"Twenty-four/seven?" he asked.

"That will be your call. If they're living their lives in a predictable routine, twenty-four/seven surveillance may not be needed. I trust your people to know when extra manpower is called for."

Max said, "Static surveillance is forty dollars an hour, mobile is at least seventy, more if it requires a three-car team. Covert or undercover operations, or the installation of monitoring equipment, is sixty per hour, plus an additional one fifty survey/setup charge, plus the cost of the equipment. Special jobs may cost anywhere from five hundred to a thousand more, depending on the level of risk it places on my operatives. I will need a retainer of seven thousand dollars, which may go quickly in this case. Pretty soon you may be looking at a per diem charge of three grand or more."

My Antioch stash of currency was going fast, but I sensed things were coming to a head. I had little time to debate costs.

"Fine. I'll give you the names and addresses of the subjects within twenty-four hours. Begin surveillance as soon as possible after I give you that information. I need daily reports and immediate contact if anything seems unusual. There is a girl missing and I want her found alive."

Max crossed his arms. Uh-oh, something else was coming. "Look, my rates are pretty damn cheap, and I have some of the best operatives in the world. But there's one caveat. They don't testify. They *never* talk to the police. And that goes for the evidence they collect, too. You won't have shit for a court case, understand? Most of my folks have a difficult relationship with the INS. You don't like this, just turn around and leave right now. I'll forget you exist."

That wasn't so bad. If he only knew whom he was talking to! I said, "No problem. As far as the Man is concerned, you don't exist."

Max reached in his desk drawer, pulled out a pager, and tossed it to me. "Whenever we get anything, we'll let you know right away. Regular reports will be e-mailed to you. They will come from hotmortgages.com and the subject line will be, 'Maximize your mortgage investments today!' Got it?"

I slipped the pager into my pocket, "Cute, nothing to trace back to you. I got it."

I was going to have to carry my pager, cell phone, a Dick Tracy wristwatch, and a portable television before this whole gig was over. Soon I was going to be a walking advertisement for Sharper Image.

I pulled up my pants leg, unstrapped a leg pocket security wallet from my calf, and counted out Max's retainer.

He smiled. "I hope the girl makes it. Give Isabel your contact information, including your e-mail address. You'll be getting reports once a day. Tell our mutual friend I said hello." I was dismissed.

I walked out of his office with an odd sense of calm. I didn't know if this was going to do any good. I might be flushing twenty thousand dollars right down the drain. But I knew I had damn good people working on my side. Mr. Murderer had better look out. I was coming toward him.

CHAPTER FIFTEEN

I headed toward the Oakland hills. I wanted to make my calls from my favorite hideout, a tree in the Mountain View Cemetery.

I love graveyards. They're the greenest, quietest places in the city. No Frisbees, no screaming babies, no rock and roll. The only music you hear is the song of the wind as it rustles the new leaves of the oak trees, accompanied by the regular beat of sprinklers and an occasional police siren wailing through the city below.

As usual, I shied away from the Tudor chapel and the massive Greco-Roman mausoleum. I steered clear of Victorian Gothic tombs perched haughtily on the top of the hill, looking down on San Francisco Bay. Resting places of dead rich people didn't appeal to me. I headed out beyond the high-rent district, beyond the groomed, wisteria-covered walkways and the smoothly paved main drives.

A rutted asphalt road wandered into the scruffy, neglected borderland of the graveyard. A short wall sheltered by a grandfather oak defined my special island. This ancient tree was far older than the park that had grown up around it. It stretched its massive, scarred arms over a small circle of graves, shading both living visitors and dead residents.

I looked around to make sure I was alone. Then I climbed up on a crumbling gravestone and hoisted myself onto a well-muscled branch. A two-minute climb brought me to my favorite crook, where a huge branch jutted out from the trunk, screening me from any passersby below. My sanctuary.

You probably think it's stupid for a fifty-five-year-old man to be climbing trees. We're supposed to be watching the Fox Sports Channel from our Sanyo massage chairs while we munch on Doritos and slowly rot. Unfortunately, I can't afford such pleasures. I need to be ready to run at any time.

I was the last revolutionary guerrilla out there. The Family got wiped up after the Brinks job. The SLA was history. The rest of the Weather Bureau had settled into comfortable lives: teaching in law schools or community colleges, doing a little neighborhood organizing, or just buying mutual funds and waiting to retire.

But my body had never been found in the rubble. All that the Man had was my blood-soaked jacket with my wallet in the inside pocket. No body, no closure. My case was very cold, but I guessed that my FBI file was still marked "Open—Inactive—Investigation Not Concluded."

So I jogged a six-mile circuit two nights a week at Cesar Chavez Park. I drove over to the city and scaled the indoor climbing structures at Mission Cliffs once a week. I trained with Maya Layton, the sensei and fifth-degree black belt at the Albany Aikido dojo on Tuesday and Thursday. And I climbed trees whenever I felt like it.

I flipped open my cell and took the one voice mail off it.

Sally was great. I jotted down the addresses and phone numbers that she had unearthed. Nothing yet on Hal, the ex-boyfriend with the active middle finger.

I called Max's receptionist and gave her the information Max would need to begin his surveillance. Now it was time to reach out and touch someone. Raise dust if I could.

Frank Wellington was probably at work. He owned a business called Diablo Investments in Walnut Creek. Everything in that area of Walnut Creek was Diablo this or Diablo that. The whole valley lay under the shadow of Mount Diablo, a large, boring peak that usually wore a small cloudy cap.

I got the man himself. Sally must have scored the inside line to his office. "Wellington, here." His voice conveyed a desire to get on with it.

"Mr. Wellington," I began, "this is Warren Ritter. I'm afraid I was one of the last persons to speak to your wife. I met her in Berkeley the day she disappeared. I'm very sorry for your loss. I'm also concerned about your daughter, as you must be. I wanted to meet with you and—"

He interrupted me, "Yes, Louise told me about meeting you. It seemed you eased her mind about Heather quite a lot. I appreciate that. Do you have any idea who might have killed her, or where my daughter is?"

I could hear the strain in his voice. I was no help, but I did want to see him face-to-face. So I lied. "I don't have any idea where she is right now, but your wife told me something interesting in the call she made to me the night she disappeared. I haven't wanted to share it with the police until I talked about it with you."

Silence on the other end. I went on, "I would like to meet with you in person to talk about this."

"Could you tell me what it is right now?"

"I'm in Berkeley, not that far away. Is tomorrow at noon convenient with you? I can come out to your office."

He said, "There's just a lot of pressure on me right now. I'm afraid Wednesday is booked. How about Thursday at noon?"

"That will be fine."

Click. He hung up on me. Strange.

I was getting stiff up there. I began climbing down and jumped the last five feet. Ouch. I hated getting older. Looking up I saw that high clouds had flown in from the south and were beginning to veil the sun. A cool breeze came up the hill from the pond below. The weather was changing. I'd better get this last call done and head home.

I called the number for Curtis.

"Yo," he said.

"Is this Curtis Jackson?"

"Who wants to know?"

"My name is Warren Ritter. I was the tarot card reader that Heather Wellington saw just before she was abducted."

"So? What're you calling me for? You with the police? They just called me ten minutes ago. You know I don't need this shit!"

"Believe me, I'm *not* with the police. Heather gave me your name" (okay, a little lie, but for a good cause). "I'm trying to find out where Heather is. I want to get together and talk with you."

He said, "Her old man hired you, didn't he? You're a private investigator. Take it somewhere else."

"Look, some people have called me a professional liar before, those folks who are not fans of the occult. But nobody has ever accused me of being a private dick. Heather called you Curly. Does that convince you I'm who I say I am."

"So what the hell do you want, Mr. Fortune-Teller?"

I needed to make this a little more personal. I said, "Look, I know you care about her."

"I wish I never met the bitch," he muttered.

"You're lying. Cut the gangsta crap with me. I know you're a nice guy and that she liked you a lot. I'm just someone who knows Heather and wants to help. She told me some stuff about you. I'd rather talk with you about it first and avoid talking to B-town's cops. Can we do it?"

"Yeah, sure, whatever. But just so you know, if you be lying to me I will fuck you up proper, nice guy or not."

"Hey, no problem."

Curtis suggested, "How about Wednesday night, Grand Lake?"

Damn, I had my appointment with Rose on Wednesdays. I said, "Thursday, six P.M., at the Cheese Steak Shop on Lakeshore, I'm buying."

"Big spender. Sure, see you then." We both hung up like polite, civilized people.

This was more than enough for one day. I headed for the entrance gate.

Walking through the cemetery, I looked around. It was getting colder, windier, and grayer. I realized that there were a lot of dead people all around me. I usually related to this place as a private park. But these are the temple grounds of death.

I wondered what my dad's grave looked like. I thought about what I would want on my gravestone. Robert Frost's was pretty good: "I had a lover's quarrel with the world." I thought mine might be, "You can run, but you cannot hide." I pulled my jacket tighter around me and hurried toward my car.

CHAPTER SIXTEEN

During the night, one of those hit-and-run rainstorms came in. The wind shook my windows like a fourth-grade schoolteacher grabbing an insubordinate student by the shoulders. I didn't sleep worth a damn.

The storm spent itself by daylight. I had no desire to vacuum, stretch, meditate, or do anything but inject caffeine into my circulatory system as soon as possible. I crawled into jeans, a sweatshirt, and a jacket. Then I put the two cell phones and pager in my pocket. I didn't know why I kept carrying around Louise's cell. I think it was sort of a talisman, to help remind me of this sweet lady who didn't deserve her fate. I headed for Caffé Med, my Mecca.

Coming back after three lattes, I stopped off at Northside Postal Services to see if Sally had scored me any data yet. It was a narrow hole-in-the-wall. Postboxes lined the walls and a bored clerk sat at a counter at the other end of the room, reading a Stephen King paperback. Box 31 was an oversized box on the bottom row near the front. When I opened it, I saw why it needed to be oversized. It contained two large packages. I took them and left. The clerk had never looked up.

Walking down Euclid toward my apartment building, I spotted trouble parked on the front stoop. The rising hair on the back of my neck told me that the man waiting on the steps in front of the leaded-glass door was a raptor.

He was dressed in a navy, tropical wool, two-button suit. Judging from his build, his jacket didn't need padded shoulders. As I got closer I noticed his shirt's European button-down collar, the highly polished Italian slip-on shoes, and the navy-and-black, tight-checkered power tie. His short, razor-cut blond hair was starting to thin out in front. Slate-blue eyes. Strong, pugnacious jaw. Thin lips.

I bet he had thick chest hair. This was a real man. He had the elevated testosterone to prove it. He looked like a cop but was too well dressed. Probably a fed. God, do I have to start every day talking to a pig?

He was hunting me. He started toward me as I crossed the street. "Are you Warren Ritter?"

Ah, the temptation to deny the accusation. But I was playing hardball, not running for the hills. I came right back at him. Walking in too close to his personal space, I smiled and practiced Curtis's line, "Who wants to know?"

"I'm Special Agent David Stiles, with the Federal Bureau of Investigation. I'm investigating the Wellington kidnapping and homicide."

"May I see some ID?" I was still wearing that I-love-authority smile. I didn't doubt that he was exactly who he said he was, but I'd never got this close to a federal shield before. I was curious to see what it looked like.

He handed me a thin, black leather case. Inside was a small gold badge with an eagle on the top. Facing it was a photo ID from the Federal Bureau of Investigation, bearing all sorts of official-looking insignias.

"Kinda tiny for a badge, isn't it?" I asked.

"We don't need to impress anyone with the size of our badges," he said coldly.

As he retrieved his badge, he handed me his business card complete with the FBI logo, his name, agency ID number, an 800 phone number, and an e-mail address. The letters and logo were embossed in gold on a heavy white cardstock. A keepsake for sure!

"I have a few questions I'd like to ask you. Do you mind if we step inside and talk?"

Playing Mr. Good Citizen is one thing, but letting the Man inside my living quarters is completely unacceptable. He'd need a search warrant for that. Instead I said, "I'd be more comfortable chatting over a decaf latte. Why don't we talk at my favorite café, Brewed Awakenings? You can find me there almost every morning. It's right down the block."

He didn't like the idea one bit. But I guess he didn't have a warrant to break into my apartment, because he started walking with me.

I hated Brewed Awakenings. It's always upbeat, warm, and friendly. Classical music in the background. Comfy couches in the back.

It was a hangout for all the defrocked priests and renegade Baptists who taught up the street at the Graduate Theological Seminary. We locals called the seminary "Holy Hill." The theological students referred to it among themselves as "Holy Hell."

Faculty and students cloistered together at this joint to mainline caffeine and deconstruct Christ.

Sam, the Palestinian owner, smiled and greeted us with an amiable, "Good morning!" We got our drinks and I headed for the sofas. I knew that Dave the fed would be uncomfortable sinking down into those overstuffed cushions. It might wrinkle the perfect crease of his slacks.

Dave began the interrogation with, "How is it that the deceased was carrying your card in her purse?" Great social skills, that guy.

It went on like this, him probing and taking notes, me trying not to get too snotty. I didn't tell him anything he didn't already know. He knew about the late-night phone call. He wanted to go over every word of that call and every detail of my two face-to-face encounters with the Wellington ladies.

He seemed fascinated about my lack of an alibi for Sunday night and Monday. He kept repeating questions in a slightly altered form, trying to catch me in an inconsistency. Having no alibi made it easier. I didn't have complex lies to remember.

He was incredulous that I could spend so long in my apartment without talking to anyone. Extroverts know nothing about the joys of solitude. Of course I didn't mention my noon expedition to the Secret Path.

One interaction bothered me a lot. I asked, "You know, Dave, I have cooperated with the authorities as much as I could. In fact, I'm taking time out of my busy day to talk with you. Why are you so interested in me? I'm not a suspect, am I?"

"At this time you are on the short list of people very closely connected to this crime. I hoped our conversation might take you off that list. Now tell me again exactly what Mrs. Wellington told you in that last call."

Under any other circumstances I would have asked to talk to my lawyer and sent him packing. But I needed to know what he knew, and his interrogation helped me figure that out.

Finally, Davie got tired of asking the same questions. He switched his tactics and started asking about my personal history. I knew the background of the character I had created. I had Warren Ritter's history down cold. Twelve years ago I had lifted his identity from an indigent whom I found frozen to death, or pickled to death, in a Chicago alley. I stole the stiff's wallet.

I had a private investigator find out everything there was to know about poor Warren. Then I memorized the details of his extremely boring life and became him. Not hard, since prior to his demise I couldn't find any record of him ever being fingerprinted. Chicago was too close to Warren's old stomping grounds, so I moved to California.

I was reciting my inventive life story, enriching it with names and addresses of the people in the past decade who could vouch for me being Warren. Dave wrote everything I said down in a wicked little black leather notebook. But when he started asking me about my best friend back in Abraham Lincoln High School, I figured enough was enough.

"I'm not sure exactly what this has to do with the Wellington investigation. You sound like you're vetting me to join the diplomatic corps. I told you everything I know."

"The scope of my investigation extends far beyond this kidnapping. I insist that you continue to answer these questions. It is a matter of national security, and I am more than willing to bring you into custody to get the information I need."

If he played the homeland security card, he wouldn't even need a judge's order to pack me away for as long as he wanted. I was very glad I hadn't followed my first instinct and I'd kept myself from spitting on his highly polished Armanis.

"Fine, Dave, no problem. I admit it, I skipped last period throughout most of my senior year to go out and drink booze."

Unamused. "Tell me about Foster Crayton."

Uh-oh. I'd Googled into the Lincoln High School alumni Web page and memorized a couple of names from the late Mr. Ritter's graduating class, but Foster's was not one of them. Resort to stupidity! "Never heard of him."

Dave smiled. He had me now. "Actually, it has been reported to me that Foster and you were best of friends."

Offense time. "Look, I don't know about you, Mr. Stiles. But I hated high school. Since graduation day I have tried to forget anyone and everyone who reminded me of those miserable years. So, sorry, but I have no idea who this Crayfish person is."

"Foster Crayton is associated with providing arms to extremist militia groups. He was rotund, dark haired, and walked with a slight limp. Does that help refresh your memory?"

I had to use what ammo I had. "No. I have no contact with the thugs and sadists who were my old classmates. And if it was Polly Tittle who told you about my deep friendship with Foster, she was the biggest liar in Illinois and hated my guts."

"I am not at liberty to discuss my sources."

Exit time. I said, "Well, I'm sorry I can't help you. I hope you catch the creep. I think I've adequately answered all your questions. We've been nursing these espressos for an hour, and I need to go back to my apartment and make several nonurgent calls. If that's all right with you?"

Dave did not smile. He was a very serious man doing a very important job. Just ask him. He said, "Fine. Please stay in the area in case I have additional questions for you. If you have any plans to leave Berkeley, call me first and leave a forwarding address and phone number."

"No problem, Dave. I'd be glad to. Contact me any time if you have any further questions." I was so nice!

I picked up my two envelopes and got up to leave. Boy, would he have been interested in seeing what was inside them! He was still brushing off his slacks as I left the brick building and headed home.

Just my damn luck. Warren Ritter, that stiff in Chicago, had to be palsy with a frigging terrorist. Ironic considering my history. But still a pain. I knew Dave would spend the next few days verifying my story. If any part of my biography rang false, he'd be right in my face. In a perverse way he was now working for me, testing my alias with all the tools of the United States government behind him. I wasn't going to lose any sleep over it.

Now I was supposed to swing into action and find the killer. The Valdez surveillance reports were piling up unread in my e-mail box. Sally's reports from Danville were unopened. But inside my apartment, I crashed. I just sat at my dining-room table and watched puffy clouds travel inland.

I was exhausted after my encounter with Dave. I don't have the stamina I had thirty years ago, running down the streets of Chicago just ahead of a phalanx of Tac Squad storm troopers. I felt lethargic. I couldn't move. Everything just seemed so pointless.

Why not let the cops do what they get paid to do. Who was I to think that I could be a crime stopper? Tarotman, with his cape in tatters, unable to leap up from his dining-room table. Some superhero!

Who am I kidding? I'm just a washed-up old ex-hippie. A few days ago my life was ordered. I wanted that back. Warren, let go of the heroics. Get your life back to normal before it gets so messy that you have to split this town and start over. It's time to call it quits.

I sat looking out the window at the clock tower, watching the hands slowly revolve. I was too tired, and too sad, to do anything else.

CHAPTER SEVENTEEN

At three I managed to creep out of my pity pot and make it downstairs to get a Top Dog from the local hot dog shop and pick up my mail. Nothing new in box #31. My own mailbox held an assortment of bills, credit card applications, and a letter from my sister. She'd addressed it to "Warren Ritter."

Dear Richard:

I appreciated you not defending yourself at our meeting. I didn't appreciate your letter. You're hardly a helpless victim of circumstance. It would have been better for you to stand up and take the punishment that was due you for your crime rather than running like a coward. I'm just glad Dad never found out you were still alive. It was bad enough to know his only son turned out a commie who blew himself up. It would have been much worse for him to know you were a fugitive for decades.

Richard, writing heartfelt phrases like "you deserved a much better brother than the one you got" isn't going to do the trick. You fucked up royally! It's going to take a lot of time and some real amends from you before I even consider writing you again. Amends aren't saying, "Gee, I'm sorry I screwed with your love and trust. Please love and forgive me!"

I'm in a twelve-step program. I've had to make amends to the people I have harmed. My sponsor gave me this rule, one you need to take to heart. She said, "Amends aren't made with words. They're made with actions. Treat the person you have hurt in a new and kinder way, and perhaps you might heal the wound you created."

Perhaps not, also. Don't think sending me flowers can unwind your twisted past. Don't write me any more nice letters. Show me.

Tara

Amends. As if I could perform a gracious good deed and all the suffering I'd inflicted on others would be magically lifted. I didn't think so. I could spend the rest of my life serving Tara and it wouldn't make a dent in the wound. Nope, there were no quick fixes for this mess.

I decided to walk across campus and have a beer at Larry Blake's, a hamburger joint with aspirations of being a historic Berkeley landmark. Alcohol made a lousy antidepressant, but I didn't have the energy to think of anything more holistic.

As I was walking through the plaza, I ran into a huge crowd of students. Someone had a megaphone. The signs read, "U.S. OUT OF THE MIDEAST," "DETHRONE THE EMPEROR," "WE NEED A REGIME CHANGE!" and "WE ARE THE TERRORISTS." I stopped for a while to listen to the speaker. Nothing new. No call to action. Just wave your signs and think you're making a difference.

I remembered carrying those signs three decades ago. And I

remembered much more. The tinge of tear gas in the air. The harsh scream of sirens as the Man tried to surround us. The thud of a nightstick as it bashed against my shoulder.

It was so different back then. In '69 we knew who we were at war with: the U.S. government. Mayor Daley had a "shoot-to-kill" order out for looters (read: black men protesting injustice). Panthers Hampton and Clark had been assassinated by the Chicago police; six hundred bullets were fired into their apartment and not one fired out from it.

Dylan sang, "You don't need a weatherman to know which way the wind blows." In those days the wind was blowing bullets toward anyone who fought to stop the war machine. Assassinations were a way of life back then: JFK, Martin, Bobby, Medgar Evers, Malcolm X, twenty-seven Black Panthers, plus who knows how many Native American and Chicano activists.

We were harassed constantly by the FBI and by every local pig who found out who we were. Cops beat me up a couple of times. Our pads were regularly searched and ransacked in the process. Our cars had their tires slashed. We had to go underground or we would have been killed.

Those were good days. We let the rulers know that they weren't as safe as they thought they were. We bombed statues, mailboxes, a Washington barber shop, and we tossed bombs at the Pentagon and the Capitol. We sought to damage the icons of imperialism, not to kill people. In fact the Weather Underground never killed anyone—except ourselves, when our bomb factory exploded and blew up four of our members, including yours truly.

History has been rewritten with us cast as criminals and nutcases. Sure, our gestures ultimately had little impact. But in a perverse way, we embodied the spirit of the Revolutionary War guerrilla freedom fighters of 1776. They dared to speak and act against what they perceived as tyranny. So did we.

Back in the late sixties we were alive, angry, and ready to kick ass. What happened? We got jailed, killed, bought off, co-opted, sucked dry, and forgotten. I was the only one left uncaught.

CHAPTER EIGHTEEN

So when did you start thinking about killing yourself again?" Rose asked.

"Can't you use a more clinical term? My last therapist talked about 'suicidal ideation.' I liked that phrase a lot better," I said.

Rose said, "You fired your last therapist, Warren. Stop avoiding me. When?"

I sighed. "After meeting with Tara. The voice in my head came back. It says, 'Warren, you're a loser. What the hell do you think you're doing? You can't avenge anything. All that's going to happen is that you'll fuck things up and you'll have to move again. You're a runner. That's all you are.' Every so often I think about eating the barrel of one of my pistols.

"Last night I had a rotten night's sleep—dreams about the fly on Louise's forehead and those red steps again. Today the FBI grilled me. My sister told me to go soak my head. And I was thinking about the old days, before I started to run. Someday I will tell you that story. Maybe. Anyway, I came here so you can fix me."

"Did you vacuum, today?" Rose asked.

She knew me way too well. "No. I watched time pass."

"Do you have a gun in the apartment?"

"No. Following your sage advice I keep them in the lockup in Antioch."

"Good. Besides last night, how are you sleeping?"

"Too many dreams," I answered.

"Now, Warren, I'm going to put some facts together and you tell me if you see a pattern here. You've had manic-depressive episodes three times before in your life, twice in your twenties and once three years ago. During that episode you were convinced that the FBI was trailing you. You changed your mind only after you went on medication to stabilize your moods. Valproate acid, as I recall."

"Rose, it's called bipolar, rapid cycling, or cyclothymia these days. 'Manic-depressive' is an antique term. It belongs in the same dust bin as 'nervous breakdown' and 'neurotic.' Try to keep up." I grinned at her.

Rose didn't smile. "You always get nasty when you get depressed. Thank you for your correction, Warren. It's a burden you have to bear, having a therapist who's been in practice for forty years.

"If I may continue, you talked with a sister, who thought you were dead for thirty years and wishes you were dead right now. You've discovered that you have a daughter you never knew existed who is about to give birth to your grandchild. Last week you had a client kidnapped. This week a client of yours was murdered. You discovered her body. You woke up sweating the last two nights from a dream of a fly walking across her head toward a black bullet hole. And I bet you've stopped taking your meds."

She paused after reciting this litany of misfortune to see if I had any response. She hadn't asked me a question, so I felt no need to speak. I'd wait and see where she was going.

She began again, "In response to all this, you swore vengeance. You decided you can outdo the police. You spent ten thousand dollars in one day trying to beat them to the killer. You paid for reports you don't read. Again, you believe that the FBI is on your trail. You called and annoyed two men, one of whom may be a kidnapper and murderer. And you regularly think about sticking a gun in your mouth and blowing your brains out. Does all this sound a little odd to you?"

I didn't like seeing this list of psychopathology so lucidly displayed. So, of course, I acted tough. "Yeah," I said, "it sounds completely insane. Maybe I should be hospitalized. Better yet, why don't you call the police and put me in lockup for a forty-eight-hour involuntary hold? You think this is all in my head, don't you? Just another FBI hallucination. You're full of shit, Rose. Just read the freakin' papers. This is real!"

Rose sighed. "Warren, chill. No one's trying to cart you off anywhere. I'm just curious. You've got to admit it sounds weird."

I got up and started pacing, something I do a lot in my sessions. "You can paste everything onto a nice little pastiche of pathology if you want to, but that's not what's going on. You think I'm manic. I know mania, and it's a hell of a lot more fun than this!"

Rose said, "Look, I don't care if you spend ten thousand dollars on investigators or on solid-gold tarot cards. It's not the mania that concerns me right now. What worries me is that you're contemplating suicide. I can't work with you if you're dead."

"And insurance doesn't pay for postmortem treatment."

"Warren, you don't have insurance. You pay in cash."

I laughed. "You doubt that the executors of my vast estate will continue to reimburse your services for performing psychotherapy on my corpse." I turned and started pacing again.

Rose walked over to me and turned me around so that I faced her. Then she put her hands on my shoulders. She rarely touched me in the middle of a session. I knew she meant business. "We can joke about it all night, but I do take your 'suicidal ideation' very seriously. So what are you going to do about wanting to kill yourself?"

I was busted. "Okay, okay. I confess. I stopped taking the meds three weeks ago. I wanted to see if I could do it by myself. I don't happen to think that what I'm going through has anything to do with my mental illness. But I see your point, it does sound strange. So here's what I'm going to do. I'm still going to get the bastard who killed Louise. But I'll go back on Depakote. I'll go home and take my first pill right now. Maybe it will help me sleep. Satisfied, boss lady?"

She smiled. "Very satisfied. Will you set up an appointment next week with Dr. Varner to make sure your blood levels are okay?"

"That old fart? Sure, that's a big ten-four, good buddy."

Rose ruefully shook her head and said, "Thank you, Warren." Then she walked over to close the curtains. She always opened them at the beginning of our sessions and closed them to signify it was time to leave. She knew how I hated to be hemmed in. I felt pretty lucky to have Rose on my side, even though I had no intention of following through on my promises to the old bird.

CHAPTER NINETEEN

I woke up to the growl of the Number Eight bus shifting gears and lumbering up Hearst Avenue. Thank God! It rescued me from another miserable dream. All I could remember were images of dismembered body parts, fire, and a pervasive sense of threat.

I looked out my bedroom window toward the bell tower, which stood proud and phallic against a blue sky. No fog. Today was going to be a Hollywood production, bright and cheery. I closed my drapes. I felt like crap.

In the kitchen I washed down four Advil with a pint of carrot-apple juice. Then I got dressed and started doing the week's chores, all of which had been ignored while I was out playing Sherlock Holmes. Once the ibuprofen kicked in, I put on shades and headed out into the harsh brilliance of the day.

I made it to my window seat at the Med, my antidepressant latte steaming in a tall glass in front of me. As I sipped I thought about the day ahead. I doubted that I'd learn much from either Frank Wellington or Curtis the boyfriend. I wasn't a great detective; I hoped the cops would do all that. Then Sally would hack it and I'd know what was going down.

But I wanted to see those two suspects face-to-face, to smell their aftershave, check out their socks, see how they stood, sat, and shook my hand. I wanted to piss them off and see how they handled it. Being with them would help me put flesh and bones to the data I was going to be collecting.

I sat gazing out the window, mainlining my caffeine. Outside the front door, a homeless man was panhandling. He was a regular, wearing a greasy Levi's jacket, black jeans, and fairly clean Nikes that he probably snagged from a free box. He defended his primo spot from interlopers, threatening violence to any other homeless person who got too close. I found myself staring at him, noting the hole in the rear pocket of his jeans and the edge of the blue-black homemade tattoo on the part of his wrist sticking out from his jacket sleeve.

The memory of last night's nightmare suddenly flooded back. I'm sitting in a doorway with a blanket wrapped around me. My town house and all my money are burned up. I'm homeless and alone. And I am going deaf; everything is getting more and more silent. Watching that panhandler brought back the whole dream.

I looked around the café. Everyone was busy. The young professor with his casual haircut that cost $100 a month to maintain was trying to pick up a cute co-ed. The hurried yuppie legal assistant was running for the bus, desperately gripping her mocha. The aging tarot card reader watched it all, feeling superior, while his latte grew cold.

All of us were living our lives in the comfortable delusion that we were safe. Only the homeless guy was really safe. His expectations were already shattered. He knew the truth—that we all hang by a slim thread above the abyss.

Then I smiled. Corporate Amerika could toss any of us out of our job and onto the street. An unknown virus could sap our strength until we couldn't get out of bed. Our addictions and craziness could unhinge us and leave us pounding on police cars in helpless rage until the Man carted us off. But I was ready.

Job's story didn't scare me. Take it all, strip me of everything, and I would still snarl and grab for the last taste of life. Most of the good citizens around me had never been tested. They'd fold under the stress of failure. But I'd lived my life under unbearable tension. That tension had dried up any sentimental softness I might have had and left me lean, bitter, and ruthless. If I were homeless, the first thing I would do is kick that panhandler's ass and take over his lucrative spot.

I slugged down the rest of my latte and headed off to raise hell. Back in my apartment I could feel the temptation to open Sally's envelopes and start reading. But I didn't want to get derailed in details and contradictions. I didn't want my "native hue of resolution" to get "sicklied o'er with the pale cast of thought." Today was a day for action. Tonight I would do research.

Time to dress for battle. I stripped off my grungies and went to the power casual part of my walk-in closet. Working at Nordstrom had one great advantage: employee discounts. I picked an olive turtleneck, slacks that were more brown than green, and a Donegal green-and-tan-herringbone tweed sports jacket. The slip-on ostrich-skin loafers finished the ensemble perfectly. I was casual enough for Oakland and classy enough for

Walnut Creek. One thing I didn't look like was a Telegraph Avenue tarot card reader.

Then I went to the medicine cabinet to adjust my blood chemistry. Here's a short course on bipolar mood swings. The down cycles suck. Hamlet lives in each of us. We all "grunt and sweat under a weary life." Who hasn't thought about prematurely ending "the heartache and the thousand natural shocks that flesh is heir to"? Suicide can look damn attractive as you're falling into the pit. The trick was to avoid killing myself during my downswings.

But unlike the rest of humanity, we rapid-cycling bipolars get rewarded for making it through hell. The upswing is reserved for a privileged few. Imagine the happiest day of your life. You were brilliant, and everyone loved you for it. You found love, recognition, fortune, triumph. There's a tarot card, the Six of Wands, that portrays a hero riding back home bearing the flag of victory. Remember that kind of day?

Now multiply it by ten and you get close to what we bipolars get to feel as we soar up out of our depression: joy, intense aliveness, a sharpening of all our senses (and I do mean all of them), brilliant thinking, freed-up imagination, unclouded vision. Mystics write about heightened states of consciousness and call it enlightenment. We manics get to taste that nectar regularly. We live for it.

The art of being bipolar is to ride the wave up without losing control. I knew better than to take an antidepressant. That could skyrocket me into a full-blown manic state of wild aliveness. I could really make a mess of things. I had to ease into the high.

I'd begin by taking my mood stabilizers at a quarter dose. I'd maintain a low dosage until I felt the positivism start to fade. Then I'd stop the stabilizers and start the antidepressants. Sometimes I could kick-start the upswing again. That part of the ride was rougher, with bigger swings and a final drop.

Rose was my rudder on this journey. She'd tell me if I was getting too extreme in one direction or another. Then I could adjust the meds to chill.

She didn't always know that she was serving this purpose. These cycles happened a lot more often than I ever told Rose. I don't think she'd approve of the ways I self-medicated to milk the high. Besides, I had been involuntarily hospitalized once, a long time ago, when I trusted a therapist too much. I wasn't going to let it happen again.

Rose was off base this time, though. Going after Louise's killer wasn't manic grandiosity. I was pissed. I wasn't going to be driven out of this town. Right now I needed that manic brilliance. I needed to shift into high gear to beat this guy.

I logged onto my AOL account. Cher's voice greeted me with "Hi Babe." First, I went to Yahoo to print out a map to the address Sally had given me for Wellington's office. Then I went to my e-mail account and saw that I had seven new e-mails. Two of them promised that my genitals would be massive in weeks if I used their product. One wanted me to know that I could buy any drug I wanted without a doctor's prescription. One offered access to a 24/7 live camera trained in the bedroom of hot young coeds. Two of them were from hotmortgages.com. I decided to read Max's reports tonight. And one, from an unfamiliar address, Lorilee638@hotmail.com, read, "Ripley alert." I opened it:

```
Package One delivered.
31747
34134
514709
```

Sally had stolen passwords for hundreds of e-mail accounts and used them randomly to deliver her messages. The column of numbers meant that she wanted to speak to me. She'd taught me her code months ago. I wrote out the string of numbers in one line, deleted the first three and last three numbers, and then read the remaining numbers backward. That gave me the phone number I was to call.

I walked outside and crossed the street to the phone booth in the courtyard of the local pizza parlor. As I stepped in, I looked around the edges for any FM transmitters. The booth looked clean. I glanced around to make sure no one was watching me, and then I dialed her number. Usually when I do this I get a voice mail message recorded just for me. But this time I heard a couple of clicks, and then there was the real Sally saying, "Hello." We both knew better than to use our names. I said, "Hey, I'm impressed. I got through to the real McCoy."

She said, "Yes, McCoy here. I've got a new system. Did everything arrive?"

"I can't wait to kick off my shoes, snuggle into my armchair, and settle down for a good read."

She said, "My thawing project is over. I'd like to see you. Is tomorrow noon okay?"

I knew that "tomorrow noon" was another one of her codes. She taught me to always add two hours to any appointment she made on the phone. This chick was more paranoid than I was. An endearing quality. But Friday afternoon wasn't going to work, because I was playing hooky from the Ave and going shooting with my cop buddy. Maybe later in the evening. I translated the time into her code and said, "How about five o'clock tomorrow, right after work?"

"Great, so long!" Click. No call with her lasted more than a minute and a half.

I felt . . . well, how did I feel? Excited, scared. This was a first. Sally never called just to chat. The only times she contacted me was to get a reading. This sounded social.

I liked Sally. And I was attracted to her. She was electric, risky, and very bright. It was curious that becoming her client somehow kicked things over into a friendlier arena. I wondered what it would be like to make love to someone who was paralyzed. Knowing her, improvisation would be an art form.

Or was I just imagining things? It might have nothing to do with us. Maybe it was just about my project. Oh, well, a guy could dream. Pull out of it, dude! Wake up! Time to move.

CHAPTER TWENTY

D riving to Contra Costa County was like participating in a symbolic rebirthing ritual. First you enter the dark birth canal known as the Caldecott Tunnel. In its depths you release all the sins you might have picked up in Berkeley: global consciousness, diversity awareness, and any anticapitalist radical tendencies.

Then you emerge into a new day, where trees line the streets of Orinda, Moraga, and Lafayette, lush lawns separate the estate houses, six-lane freeways connect upscale malls, even the help drives BMWs, and everybody is clean, rich, white, and comfortable.

It's like waking up in a Muzak world, where the horror of AIDS and the Twin Towers never happened.

Residents in these communities have an effective method of slum control. You couldn't buy a garage here for less than $600,000. The slums were located down on the hot valley floor, far away from these higher elevations. Light, nonpolluting industry, high-tech start-ups, and companies servicing larger corporations had built up the northern part of Walnut Creek. That's where I was headed.

Two Corte Real Plaza was a vine-covered, four-story postmodern building, trying to blend a Santa Fe look with concrete, steel, and glass, and failing utterly. It looked like an ugly brown box attacked by parasitic ivy.

I entered the unguarded lobby and looked up Diablo Investments. Then I took the elevator to the fourth floor and waded through the plush carpet to the door at the end of the hallway. Penthouse suite, very impressive.

Tan leather chairs and a matching leather settee made the reception area cozy and inviting. Anyone comfortably encased in a six-figure salary could relax in style until he was ushered into the inner sanctum to decide which strip-mining company to invest in. In the lounge he could peruse *Yachting, Islands, Gold Digest, The New Yorker,* or *Fortune,* all artfully spread out on the mahogany coffee table awaiting his reading pleasure.

An ice-blond administrative assistant who would make a great counselor for a Nazi youth camp asked politely, "May I help you?"

"I have a noon appointment with Mr. Wellington," I said in my most proper, arrogant, rich man's tone.

She consulted the pad on her desk, "Mr. Ritter?"

"Yes. Please let him know I'm here." I was acting like a Very Important Person.

It worked. "I'll let him know right away. Please have a seat."

I moved toward the chairs, waiting to see if she would use the intercom or go on in.

I was in luck. She gracefully ascended to a standing position, supported by knockout legs. Then she glided to a door to her right, opened it, left the room, and closed the thick wooden door behind her. Perfect.

Time to play Nancy Drew. I moved over to her desk and leafed through that appointment calendar she'd been consulting. Wellington had been out Monday but back at work on Tuesday. One day of grief, and then right back into his packed schedule. A really emotional guy. I saw a letter he had signed. He used an affected little tent-top slash to cross the "t" in "Wellington." I didn't recognize his client's name.

I was back standing by the table with a copy of *Architectural Digest* in my hands when the door opened and Frau Gatekeeper told me I could enter the inner temple.

Frank Wellington's office had a great view. It was designed so that Frank could look out across the valley to Mount Diablo, while his clients could enjoy the view of him sitting behind his massive rosewood desk. One wall was covered with bookcases.

Wellington rose to greet me. He looked surprised. "All suffering comes from unmet expectations," as Buddha reminds us. Or maybe it was Oprah. Anyway, this guy had expected me to look the part of a Berkeley street person. His preconception did not jibe with my elegant but understated attire. Good. I started with a small advantage.

He shook my hand and then gestured to the chair. "Take a seat."

Control strategy number one: Don't do what they expect. I turned and inspected his bookcase. A lot of clean, new books on investing, law, and real estate. One anomaly, though, a shelf full of random titles: a few well-worn paperback mysteries, *Timetables of History, Shadow Dancing in the USA, Acting Is Believing, Men Are from Mars:* not titles for rampaging capitalists. And these weren't window dressing. He probably even read those books.

He was a little testy at my lack of obedience. "If we could get this over with soon, I have an important call coming in. Please sit down."

I didn't like the feng shui of the room, with him getting the great view and me looking at wood paneling. I moved my chair to the side of the desk so that I could look at him and at his glorious view.

Frank was a tall, aristocratic-looking man with football shoulders. His once-dark hair was thinning toward baldness. With his sharp nose and close-set eyes, you wouldn't cast him as King Arthur, more like a burly sheriff of Nottingham. He was enthroned behind a five-hundred-pound block of rosewood thinly disguised as a desk. The only items on that shiny, auburn surface were a multibuttoned phone and a Lucite block with a perfectly preserved American flag rippling in the wind inside of it. Gag me.

I continued on the offensive. "Mr. Wellington, I know you're wondering why I set up this meeting. I said something in my phone call to you that piqued your curiosity enough for you to insert me into your very busy schedule—"

He interrupted me. "Yes, and please get to the point. This murder, and the kidnapping of my daughter . . . I really don't have much of a capacity for chitchat with a gypsy, or whatever you are. What did Louise say to you?"

He seemed like a very nice guy. I couldn't imagine him kidnapping his daughter and killing his wife. But my list of suspects was embarrassingly small. I'd read all those hard-boiled private eye novels and they always did these interviews. Now that I was here, I really didn't have the slightest idea what to do next. I decided to find out some more about his relationship with Heather. I ignored his question and asked one of my own.

"When I was talking with Heather, she said that you disapproved of her boyfriend. What specifically didn't you like about him?"

"Look, Mr. Rudder—"

"That's Ritter."

"Whatever. I'm not here to answer your questions. You said you had something to tell me, so please do it."

This wasn't going like Nero Wolfe. He wasn't going to give me anything. What was I doing here? The poor guy was in grief, working like a dog, and I was bugging the shit out of him.

"I'm sorry. I'm wasting your time. I'll leave now."

He blew. "What the hell is this all about? What's your game? Tell me what Louise told you, or get the hell out of here!"

I took the second option. I got up and walked out. Nodding to Ms. Hitler, I fled out the mahogany door and into the hall. I resolved to stick to fortune-telling.

CHAPTER TWENTY-ONE

I'd had enough of white bread. It was time to go back to the land of multiseeded, whole-grain, sourdough baguettes.

I emerged from the tunnel to one of the most beautiful sights on the planet. Before me Berkeley/Oakland cascaded down to the shore, a metallic net of houses, buildings, and highways. Beyond the cities, the blue-silver expanse of the bay sparkled like a promise.

Across the bay, San Francisco was just throwing off a mantilla of wispy fog and getting ready to soak up the afternoon sun. "Breathtaking" is such an overused Madison Avenue kind of word. But here it was an understatement. If there was a Creator, she manufactured the universe just to perfect this vista.

My resolve to concentrate on the arcane arts faded as I came back home. I decided to try the detective thing one more time. After all, it couldn't get much worse than that last interview.

I had four hours to kill before dinner with Curtis in the Grand Lake district. That was enough time to circumambulate Lake Merritt and to go to some bookstores. The lake is a man-made, landlocked estuary with bay water pumped into it. Lake Merritt was once an arm of the bay. In the 1800s they filled in the neck and cut it off from the bay. Then a clever developer sold the new real estate they just created. The brackish pond is belted by parkland and ringed with graceful retro streetlamps that light it up like a jeweled necklace at night.

I kicked off my loafers and put on a pair of New Balance running shoes. It's a pleasant three-and-a-half-mile jog around the lake. It wasn't long or grueling enough to raise a sweat. Considering that I was the best-dressed runner on the asphalt path, it was just as well that I wasn't sweating like a pig. Keeps the dry-cleaning bills down.

Then I headed off to Walden Pond, a good local bookstore. I hang out in bookstores. I'd like to die in Berkeley's Black Oak Books just so my ghost could continue to check out the rare books section.

Five years ago I collected two hundred signed poetry books during one of my manic phases. After coming down, I realized that books were a dangerous anchor. I might need to fade away in a hurry, and I didn't want to have to worry about my 1927 signed first edition of Robinson Jeffers's *The Women at Point Sur*.

So all my books went back to Black Oak to be traded in. Now I have only seven books in my apartment at any one time, none of them worth more than $50. If I want to bring in a new one, I have to give away an existing book. I go through two to three books a week that way. This system emptied my bookshelves and kept my life much more manageable.

You'd think libraries would provide the perfect solution for me. Thousands of books just waiting to be read. But I hate libraries like I hate zoos. Books are defaced, marked, sorted, and trapped on their shelves, prisoners forever. Books need to be owned, cherished, and then given away as gifts. Not ensnared in indentured servitude until they fall apart.

I realized that my beliefs were politically incorrect. Libraries provided books to those who could not afford them. It was stupid to attribute human characteristics to these inanimate objects. But I still imagined that the books felt like helpless prisoners on library shelves. It doesn't end there. I also imagined that books are happy in bookstores. It's like a pet store. They eagerly wait for the right owner to come along.

In bookstores I wander free, looking for old, unusual, or flat-out bizarre books. I read for hours, either on one of the rare benches or plopped down on the floor, propped up against a shelf. Folks walk around me. I don't go to the giant superstores where marketing consultants are constantly working on increasing aggressive flow-through. Bookstore owners, at least the owners of the independent bookstores I frequented, were patient with eccentrics like me.

I was in the third chapter of *The Fall of Berlin* by Read and Fisher when I noticed the light fading. Almost six. Damn, I was going to have to buy this book. On my way to the counter I was debating with myself, *Self, do I give Louise Glück's* The Wild Iris *to Sally, or Stephen Mitchell's* The Gospel According to Jesus *to Officer Mac?* To trim my collection down to seven, I had some tough decisions ahead.

I hurried past the Grand Lake Theater, a movie palace built in 1926 for vaudeville and the silent movies, and still charming. The Cheese Steak Shop was one of many hole-in-the-wall restaurants lining Lakeshore Avenue. I got in line behind a good-looking young black man wearing an azure cashmere sweater and black wool slacks. It was worth a try. After all, I was the psychic. I said, "Curtis?"

He turned around and looked me up and down. I must have passed muster because he nodded. I paid for both platters of cheese steak sandwiches and curly fries. We sat at a table near the rear of the narrow room, away from the grill and the other customers. He hadn't said much besides giving his order. He started eating.

I said, "How long did you know Heather?"

Curtis shook his head and finished chewing that bite. Then he said, "No, this isn't an interview. You said you had something to tell me about Heather. Speak."

I said, "You're worried about her."

He snorted. "My woman's been kidnapped, her mother's been shot dead. Hell, yes, I'm worried. Look, mister, I don't know who you are, but if you can help her, do it! Now tell me what we're doing here."

I noticed moisture at the edges of his eyes. Was he holding back tears? If he was faking it, he was a consummate actor.

I couldn't come up with a convincing cover story, so I tried the truth. "Heather loves you. She thinks you are considerate and gentle. I agree with her evaluation. I'm here to find Heather. I got into this case accidentally, but I'm not leaving it till she gets back home."

He sighed and said, "How can I help? I talked to the cops already, but they don't seem to know where to look. They want to pin it on me."

"Figures," I said. "You're young and you're black. They need look no farther. I hope you have a good alibi. You'd be a perfect fall guy for this."

He nodded. "My story ain't great, but they haven't picked me up yet. I'm waiting."

I wrote a name and number on a napkin and put it down in

front of him. "Clyde Berkowitz is a scrappy, successful criminal lawyer. Oakland prosecutors hate him and fear him. He has a sixty percent acquittal rate and he hates plea bargains. A terrible attorney to have if you're guilty but great if you're innocent. If he tries to tell you he's too busy, use my name. He'll help; he owes me one."

Curtis picked up the napkin and put it in his pants pocket. "Thanks. I may need it sooner than I think."

I'd passed some test of his. When I asked, "Now, tell me about your relationship with Heather," he laid out his story.

They met at a rave. She'd just broken up with her boyfriend. They liked each other right away and started dating. Her parents hated Curtis, or at least hated that their baby was with an evil black man from Oakland. Heather did what she wanted to do anyway and got into a lot of fights with her folks.

I said, "I think Mr. and Mrs. Wellington were idiots. If I had a daughter, I'd wish that she found someone as decent as you." *If I had a daughter?* But I didn't want to think about that.

He smiled. "You must be from Berkeley."

"What about her ex-boyfriend?" I asked.

"A real piece of shit. Abusive, both physically and emotionally. Hated the idea that she could leave him, especially for a nigger.

"He's a selective racist. Runs with a mixed brown and white gang but hates blacks. I met him once and thought he was going to take me out. One of the few times I was really glad to see an Oakland cop walk by. Heather thinks he might be stalking her."

I said, "I think I met him. Fat kid in a silver Grand Am?"

"That's his dad's car. He drives a beat-up old black Tercel."

"What's his name, besides Hal, and where's he live?"

"His name is Hal Russell and he lives in Concord."

"Do you think he snatched her?" I asked.

"He's angry enough to do it, that's for sure. According to Heather, that gang is into everything else, drugs, arson, prostitution, burglary. It wouldn't surprise me if they added kidnapping onto their list. Also they have Mob and Crip connections. The Crips are one of the two main drug-running gangs in the West."

"I know about the Crips and the Bloods, Curtis. Go on."

Curtis shook his head. "What I don't get is why they knocked off Louise. That's what's got me stumped."

I said, "Look, Curtis, I am pretty much in a fog right now. I don't even know the right questions to ask. Will you give me your phone number and address? I may have more questions in a little while. Is that okay with you?"

He ripped off a corner of the place mat and wrote his information down. Then he asked, "What about if I need to get in touch with you?"

I gave him one of my cards, the Magician, with my sticker on the bottom. I told him not to get murdered. Folks with my card seem to get in big trouble these days. He shook my hand and told me he'd be in touch if he found anything out. We parted company on the same team.

Rose says I'm a little paranoid. I call it a healthy suspiciousness. As I left the restaurant I spent a moment closely examining the store window of the clothing shop just down the street. I saw Curtis head for the parking structure behind Lucky's Supermarket. I gave it a minute and then followed him. I was just in time to see him drive out the exit in a white van. Was that the van that Heather got snatched in? Goddamn it! Had he totally conned me? He was back on the list, with a vengeance.

CHAPTER TWENTY-TWO

I went home and wrote down everything I remembered from both interviews. The more I wrote, the more excited I got. I recorded everything that had happened since Heather's tarot reading. I sketched the murder scene. I pulled out the four tarot cards that I felt were key: the Eight of Swords for Heather, Death for Louise, the King of Swords for the murderer, and the Hanged Man for me. I laid the paperwork and cards out on my dining-room table and began moving the stacks around, looking for patterns.

My back ached. I stopped and stretched. Then I examined my handiwork. It looked like a mess of trash. What was I doing? This was stupid. What a waste of time. What the hell difference did it make? I wasn't going to stop this guy. And besides, it was none of my business. Why was I giving this wild-goose chase an ounce of my energy?

I was full of bullshit. I wanted to go running down Dick Tracy Lane because I was scared to death of facing the real puzzle. I had a daughter. What was I going to do about that?

Who the hell was the mother? That's what I should be investigating, not someone else's murder. Fine, I was leaving murder to the cops. I walked away from the table and lay down on my bed with a fresh pad of yellow paper. I began to make a list. Soon I had it pared down to the four women I slept with during the window of opportunity, four months between November of '69 and February of '70. I looked at my list of candidates:

- *Wendy:* The girl who would always put out. She was a lot older than me, an ex-beatnik art student from NYU.
- *Veronique:* My on-again, off-again obsession. She was sleeping with women during most of that period, but I think we made it a couple of times.
- *Cathy:* She was an ex-girlfriend. But the two of us had one of those for-old-times-sake evenings just before Christmas.
- *Good old what-the-hell-was-her-name:* I celebrated New Year's Eve in bed with a chick whom I could barely remember. All that I could remember about her was a birthmark on her left breast in the shape of the state of New Hampshire. If she was the mom, I had no idea how to trace her. I'd be sunk.

I sat back and tried to empty my mind. I focused on my breath going in and out. Slowly the carousel of mental voices came to a halt. There was a brief moment of silence. Then I knew who the mother was.

I remembered coming back home in late February, just before everything fell apart. I had to explain unsuccessfully to my mother why I dropped out of Princeton. I was already underground, but my family didn't know it. I longed to touch my old life one last time. Mom thought I was on drugs because I was so moody, but it was just premature nostalgia.

I went to my high school and hung out across the street. I just wanted to watch kids doing the same stupid things I used to do. I walked around town. I called my old friends and got together.

Except for Cathy. She kept dodging my calls. When I did get her on the phone, she said she had the flu. That didn't ring true.

Why was she avoiding me? The night before Christmas we had a great time together. We were amazed that we could be friends, fuck, and not be upset about going our separate ways. I asked around, but the guys I knew said that she wasn't seeing anyone new.

What convinced me she was the mother of my child was a strange incident that happened on my last day in town. I ran into Vicky, a friend of Cathy's and mine. She gave me a big smile and said, "Hey, congratulations!"

I asked, "Congratulations for what?"

She looked stricken, face getting pale, and then flushed. Then she said, "Oh, I thought you . . . She . . . Oh, gosh, I've gotta go now! Bye-bye." She fled down the street away from me. I could never figure out what that encounter meant. Now I knew. Cathy had something very important to tell me but never got around to it.

It was almost midnight when I figured this out. I needed help. I didn't want to get Sally involved in this. I'm not sure why, but it was embarrassing and too personal. I didn't want her to know what a creep I was. I called the number for Valdez Security. Max himself answered.

"What the hell are you doing there so late?" I asked.

"What the hell are you doing calling me so late?" he countered.

I said, "Max, I have another assignment I'd like you to take on. It has nothing to do with this case. I'd like to keep it strictly between you and me."

"Shoot."

"I want you to find the current address of a woman, around thirty-four. She lives somewhere in Northern California, I think. She's pregnant. I don't know her name, but her mother's maiden name was Cathy Witkowski."

"Spell that last name."

I did.

Max asked, "Is that Cathy with a 'C' or a 'K'?"

"A 'C.' "

"What's her middle name?"

"Emerald."

"Okay, go on."

"Cathy was born and raised in Hopewell, New Jersey. She was still living there in 1970. Cathy would be around fifty-two or so. Can you track her daughter down?"

Max ignored my question. "What were Cathy's parents' first names?"

"Carl and Betty, I think."

"Any address?"

"They lived on Bowler Street in Hopewell, but I have no idea of the street number."

"Parents' professions?"

"Cathy's mother was a physician and her father was some sort of manager at a paint distributor, something like that."

"Brothers or sisters?"

"One younger brother Tommy, about three years younger than her."

Max took a breath. "Well, you wanted to know if I can find this lady. Before the Internet, it would have taken me about three months to tell you to forget it. Now it takes only a couple of hours to tell you to forget it. Within a week I'll know if this is a wild-goose chase or if we can dig her up. I'd say the odds are about fifty-fifty."

"Thanks, Max. And I appreciate you not asking me why I want this information."

"None of my business." He hung up the phone. Great bed-side manner, that guy.

CHAPTER TWENTY-THREE

lmost two weeks since that god-awful tarot reading and Heather's abduction. Five days since I had found Louise's body. I woke up sharp and clear. Today I was back on the hunt. I had to get Special Agent Stiles off my back and find that girl, alive or dead. I brought my latte back to the apartment and began reading Sally's notes and the Valdez surveillance reports.

God, surveillance is a boring job. I'd rather be a manager at McDonald's. The watchers deserved everything I was paying them. Imagine spending a day watching a guy go to work and come home. You can't even read an interesting book while you're waiting for something to happen. Snoresville, totally.

I realized there was too much information, and too many sources of information, to keep everything in my head or on my table. I had to see it all spread out before me. I looked around for a work surface large enough.

My bookshelf was now almost empty except for a few knick-knacks and six books. I turned it around so that the shelves faced the wall. The large blank wooden back of the bookshelf faced me. Perfect.

I started pinning up sheets of paper on it. On them I wrote, "Suspects," "Kidnapping," and "Murder." Under suspects I hung another four sheets, labeled "Frank Wellington," "Curtis Jackson," "Hal Russell," and "Someone Else." Then under each of those names I pinned up two more sheets, one marked "Motive" and one marked "Alibi."

I pulled apart Max and Sally's reports and added my notes to the stack. Then I found a pair of scissors and began cutting out significant information and pinning the fragments I chose under each section. I also hung the King of Swords over the Suspects section, the Eight of Swords over the Kidnapping section, Death over Murder, and the Hanged Man, which represented me, right in the middle.

After bomb throwing and before Chicago, I did a summer as a white-water river guide in Northern California. A place called ARTA trained me and worked my buns off all summer. I loved it.

We trained on a bunch of rivers. One day we were on the East Carson going down the same rapid five times. We would run it, haul our boats back upriver, and run it again.

At the end of the fourth run, our lead guide, a wiry woman named Shelly, said, "Okay, some of you slipped through this rapid, some of you powered through, and some of you stumbled through this run. You know it pretty well. Now I want you to track it. There is a subtle line through every stretch of the river where the water is moving effortlessly. We call that route the track. When you set your boat on the track, it slides through white water with minimal help or direction from you. The river becomes the guide.

"You can't think your way to the track. It's far too subtle for that. Your arms, the seat of your pants, and your heart are the sense organs that can put you on the track. When you're on it, not only does the boat move differently, but you feel different. Finally you are one with the river. You're not fighting your way down it anymore. You are a precious and valued part of the river as it flows."

She was right, and she was talking about a lot more than rafting. Ever since then I have looked to see if there was a track I wasn't sensing. Being manic helped me to see the fine trace of the easiest and most perfect route through things.

There's a track in tarot readings, a line that connects the powerful cards. There's a track in climbing a wall, the path of greatest flow. And there was a track through this chaos of questions. I could begin to feel it. I didn't see the destination, but I could start to sense the direction.

The surveillance reports on Curtis confirmed my initial impression: college prep all the way. He lived at home with his parents. He went to Laney Junior College during the days and worked nights at the Alameda County Animal Shelter. According to a police interview, he was there the night of the murder. I still didn't trust him. All my instincts were warning me that he was a con man. We needed to keep a close tab on him.

Not that the reports on Dickhead Wellington were any more interesting reading. Mr. Routine. No side trips to murder anyone or to write ransom letters to himself.

He was out inspecting property with a prospective investor on the afternoon Heather was kidnapped. The night Louise disappeared, he called the police, and they served as a pretty good alibi. I didn't care how good his alibis were. I was going to keep up the surveillance on him, just because I didn't like him.

I needed to get a tail on Hal, the abusive ex-boyfriend. I *really* didn't like him. I would have punched his lights out that afternoon if he hadn't sped off in his dad's car. I decided to help out my local police force. I'd give them Hal's address and let them pay him a nice little visit. But first Sally had to dig it up.

I left the apartment, walked a half a block to a plaza of restaurants. I inspected that public phone. It looked clean. I called Sally's new number, and after the clicks and hums, there was her voice. "Lancelot?"

I said, "Do you know the phone numbers to all the booths I call you from?"

"Just about."

"You're a trip, girl. I know we're seeing each other tonight, but I got more information about ex-boyfriend Hal."

"Shoot."

"He's a white, blond male in his midtwenties. His name is Hal Russell. He does indeed live in Concord, but he drives an old black Toyota Tercel. His dad drives the new silver Grand Am. I need address and phone number."

"Can do. It'll take about ten minutes. I'll leave it on your e-mail. Also, you have an new delivery."

"Great, thanks. When you get that information, will you also send it to our associate in Fruitvale?"

"Done. Looking forward to seeing you. Bye."

Click. She was gone. I smiled as I put down the receiver. Her last comment left a warm feeling in a number of places in my body.

Next I went to the booth in front of the grocery store and called Max. He was out. I told Isabel to tell Max to continue surveillance on Curtis and Frank, and to begin surveillance on

Hal Russell as soon as he received identifying information from our mutual friend. She understood.

I checked out the mailbox service. Sure enough, there was another package in Box #31. I went back to my crowded dining-room table and opened Sally's delivery.

Two hours later I finished adding her information to my evidence board. I wasn't much wiser, but I was a lot more worried. Berkeley was investigating the murder, and Danville caught the kidnapping. Curtis was their main kidnap suspect because Heather's backpack was found in an alley near his home.

That made no sense. As much as I didn't trust him, I didn't think he'd be stupid enough to toss the pack out his bedroom window while he was tying her down. He was their main suspect because he was a black man.

Danville was working with the Oakland police to determine if Curtis had gang affiliations. They were also investigating his statement as to his whereabouts during the time of the kidnapping. If his alibi didn't hang together, he was going to need that lawyer.

No ransom calls to the Wellingtons since the one that came the night Louise disappeared. That one wasn't recorded. The FBI must have been champing at the bit to be let in on this one because Special Agent Stiles was on my doorstep the day after they were called in.

The last note in Detective Flemish's case notes made my hands cold. "Berkeley homicide has hard evidence. May have perp soon. Need to coordinate interrogation." Maybe they found out who really did it. Maybe they were closing in on me.

I checked my e-mail, and sure enough, Sally had come through. She had noted that Hal's parents lived at 232 Redwood

Street and Hal lived at 232A Redwood Street. Maybe a studio or something. I wrote down Hal's address and phone number, and then called my dear friend in Danville, Detective Flemish.

Luckily I got his answering machine. I said, "Hey, Bob, Warren here. I just happened to run across the address and phone number of Hal Russell, Heather's old boyfriend. What a coincidence! I only saw him once, but he looks like a criminal type. Anyway here it is . . ." and I gave him the information.

I was having a great time with this detective stuff: building my wall of evidence, uncovering what was hidden under a rock, looking for the track that would lead to the killer.

That afternoon I was shooting it out with a cop. It was the day for target practice with Jim McNally. Self-restraint, and perhaps self-preservation, kept me from bringing up the topic of the murder. But it was weighing on me, and I was humiliated by the final score.

We drove in separate cars to Tandoori Chicken. At least I had half an hour free from his merciless teasing about my defeat. When we were sitting down to eat, I picked at my excellent Indian dinner. Mac was in rare form, offering to buy my pistol since obviously the extrapyramidal nervous symptoms from the antipsychotic medication I was taking were permanently damaging my peripheral nervous system. He knew nothing about my mental problems and was just giving me shit. But I wondered if he might be right. It was time to talk about something else.

"Speaking of psychotic," I said, "any more clues about that woman who was wasted in the park in Berkeley?" It was an awkward segue, more like jerking the conversation down the trail I wanted it to go.

Mac said, "She wasn't shot there, just dumped there. We got a break. The stupid perp stuck his fancy alligator-skin shoes in a garbage bin. An LOL saw him and thought it was suspicious. So we got a pair of fancy shoes with traces of dirt from the place where he dumped the body. Looks like the homicide occurred somewhere else. No luck on the prints or DNA."

"LOL?"

"Little old lady and self-appointed chief block watcher."

I was trying not to sweat. Unsuccessfully. "Lucky you. An eyewitness, that should help."

"Not really. She's a bust as a witness. Probably the guy was white. No ID on the car. Not sure of the perp's hair color, eyes, complexion. Just a medium-build, middle-aged guy. Hell, that could be anyone. Even you. God help us if we need her on the witness stand."

I told Mac I had a hot date later on and needed to split. He gave me more shit about my oncoming senility and its effect on eye-hand coordination. I was not amused, which pleased him even more. Damn, I was glad to be driving away from that diner.

I'd been so careful. This news was bad, really bad. But not terminal. They were going to have a lot of fun tracing those shoes. I'd shoplifted them from Nordstrom. Tomorrow some free box in Foster City was going to be the recipient of a nice pair of freshly washed Levi's and a light blue chambray work shirt. Nothing left pointing to me.

But I hated that they had my shoes. It was getting too close. I had to catch the killer very soon!

CHAPTER TWENTY-FOUR

The sun was dropping fast. I parked in front of a pizza parlor on Solano and walked along, window-shopping. I turned and strode into a narrow alley that separated the business district from the residential area of Albany. Then I walked down the street and stood under a willow, watching the streets. From where I stood it was easy to see in three directions and determine whether anyone was trailing me. I stayed there motionless for five minutes before deciding I was clear.

It was a seven-block walk to Sally's house. Strolling through the quiet neighborhood, I started to relax. The orange light of the setting sun, the blue flickering coming from living-room windows as families turned on the evening news, a dog protesting his exile from the house. Life the way ordinary people lived it.

I felt sad. I'd run from this life cluttered with mortgage payments, family dogs, and three-wheeled bikes in the driveway. I'm sure if I'd been inside one of those boxes I'd feel claustrophobic and long for freedom. Maybe.

Lighten up, Warren! I was on my way to my first date in six months. And with a gorgeous, sparkling woman who was more batshit crazy than I was, and that's saying a lot. As I neared her house, I checked again. No tail and no suspicious PG&E vans or Pac Bell trucks parked anywhere near it. Rendezvous time.

I heard her voice command, *"Vrij!"*

The door clicked, and I opened it to Ripley's rough paws, slimy tongue, and dog breath. Detaching her took a while. I knew Sally could give a command and Ripley would immediately go over and sit next to her. I also knew that nothing I could say would alter this dog's behavior one whit. Sally just laughed at my inundation and gave me no help at all.

Finally Ripley was through with me and let me enter. Sally was dressed to the teeth in a side-ruched dress with spaghetti straps. A floral print of purple roses embossed on silk climbed up her body. She gestured for me to sit next to her, where a small table was set out with puff pastry hors d'oeuvres and a fluted glass of white wine for each of us. Life was improving.

The wine was biting and astringent, with a touch of berry. Just kidding! If I haven't drunk too much, I can usually tell the difference between wine and beer, and that's about the sum of my expertise as a wine taster. This one was cold, crisp, and delicious, and I wanted a second glass. The pastry had crab and young asparagus in a cream base, and I could have finished off the whole plate and asked her to fill my dog dish with more.

Sally said, "Look, I don't want to talk any business tonight, but I have to let you know one thing. Then let's agree, nothing else about your project. This is a date, not a meeting, okay?"

"Sure. I'm sick of it anyway. What's the one thing?"

"There was a busted ransom drop today. According to Flemish's notes, a call came in early this morning. Wellington showed up with a briefcase full of cash and a team of FBI agents staking the place out. No one showed. When Frank returned to his house, a message on his machine said that the kidnappers saw that he had brought in the feds. They threatened to kill his daughter if he ever did anything like that again. He was totally pissed that the FBI somehow blew their cover. He wants them off the case."

I couldn't figure out all the ramifications of that news. Besides, I was sick to death of murder. I said, "Nice work, Sally, thanks. Okay, no more crime talk, I swear."

A brief silence blossomed. Neither of us knew what to say.

Sally spoke first. "I know plenty about Warren the man, probably more than you want me to know. But I don't know anything about you as a kid. So tell me a story about your childhood. A real story."

I thought about my walk to her house this evening. It had churned up an old memory. "Okay," I said. "I don't know if it's a story or just a scene, but I was thinking about it coming over here.

"I was thirteen, and I didn't like to stay cooped up inside my house. About a half hour after sunset I'd get on Sterling, my bike. Sterling was a big, old, one-speed clunker, spray-painted shiny silver. He had thick balloon tires, no lights or reflectors, and pedal brakes that occasionally worked.

"Sterling and I would cruise the streets. You couldn't hear anything except the whoosh of his fat tires on the asphalt and maybe an occasional rumble of sixteen-wheelers as they headed north on Route One.

"I used to love those hot summer nights. Fireflies would be blinking on and off. You could smell the newly mowed lawns. Sterling and I glided through the night.

"I'd look in on my neighbors. There was everybody eating dinner or watching TV. All tucked in for the night. And I was riding free."

This was kind of a narrative Truth or Dare game. I wondered how she would play it. I said, "Now it's your turn. Tell me about a time when your life turned a corner."

She stopped smiling. She said, "I'm not going to talk about the army." She was silent for a while. Finally, she cocked her head toward me and said, "Hey, this is a personal little exercise, isn't it. Okay, I'll tell you about the night I realized that it didn't matter whether or not there was a God.

"Eighteen, I was just out of high school and hungry for an adventure. Nobody could tell me what was safe or dangerous. I could handle anything. So I threw a bunch of clothes into the back of my red VW bug and headed for the Baja coast, all by myself. It sounded so romantic.

"Driving to the shore turned into a frightening tightrope act. I had to stay perched above crumbling ruts. I dodged tire-eating holes. I threaded my way, just guessing sometimes where the road was. And I had to hurry. The sun was setting, and if it went down, I'd be lost in the middle of a craggy, barren desert.

"The light barely held. The road finally ended at a concrete brick bar surrounded by jeeps. Mariachi music polluted the night, and raucous, drunken, big-bellied guys spilled out of the dark, smelly building and stumbled across the cold, windy beach. Paradise sucked.

"I pulled my car under a palm and waited until I thought no one was looking at my little bug. When it was dark enough, I put on my pack, hurried away from the bar, and walked along the windy surf until I couldn't hear the brass section any longer.

I threw my sleeping bag down in a partially sheltered depression in the sand and collapsed onto it.

"I hoped none of the drunken men had seen me and decided to come and rape me. I felt stupid. Here I was, alone, unknown, frightened, and cold. My images of a nurturing adventure in tropical Mexico were blown away in the unceasing wind.

"The stars came out and stared at me. I felt so little underneath their gaze. As I wrapped my bag around me, I realized that I was lying to myself.

"The stars weren't staring at me. The stars didn't see me or care about me. The black expanse of space above me was completely unaware of my existence. I mattered not at all. My insignificant life would make no impact on the passage of time or the immensity of space. The sand I lay on would last longer than my trivial existence. I was trapped in a skin shell, doomed to live a tiny life and pass unnoticed into oblivion. God, if she was out there, didn't give a rat's ass if I lived or died. I was on my own.

"That was much scarier than rape. I pulled out a bottle of tequila and drank until I fell asleep."

She smiled. "Okay, so I bared my soul, and you got away with some pissant little tale about riding your bike. Not fair! Typical of a guy, though. Let the woman expose herself, while you play it safe. So pony up, buddy. Tell me about some creepy moment in your life."

She was right. She deserved something more from me. But what story could I use? I knew I wasn't going to talk about the sixties. Not yet. So I went farther back.

"I was nine when my parents separated. It wasn't common in those days, separating and divorcing. In fact I was the first kid in my class to have his family break up. Times sure have changed.

"For weeks before Armageddon, my sister, Tara, and I had been whispering that something bad was on the way. Every night, angry voices echoed down the stairs from our parents' bedroom. Twice Dad had stormed out of the house and didn't come back for breakfast. Mom cried at weird times during the day.

"I remember once, after a midnight battle between my parents had settled down, I crawled into Tara's bed. She was three years older than me, but in that moment we were just two scared kids, curled up to each other for comfort.

"August twelfth, 1956, D-day for our family. After a silent breakfast, Dad called us into the living room. Here it comes! Merciless sunlight poured in from the front window. I sat motionless next to Tara on the faded leather couch, waiting for the worst. Mom sat in her high-backed easy chair, weeping. Dad was too nervous to sit. He paced in front of the big window, framed in drapes of blazing oranges and greens.

"Dad finally spoke. 'Your mother and I have decided to get a divorce. I'm going to be moving out of the house. I have a new job in California. Your mother has decided to stay here in New Jersey with you kids. That doesn't mean I'm going to disappear. My job entails a lot of traveling. I'll be back here often to see you. But, for now, your mother will be taking care of you. I really want you to listen to her and obey her.'

"At this point my sister lost it. She started sobbing, which only pissed Dad off. He commanded, 'Tara, please stop crying and let me finish. Stop, now!'

"She shut up. Then he turned to me. 'Richard, I want you to be a good little cowboy. You're going to have to take care of Tara and your mother while I'm gone. I'm sorry it's working out like this.'

"I didn't react. Tara was doing enough of that. She ran across the room and clutched Dad. 'Oh, Daddy, please don't go. We'll be good . . . promise!'

"I quietly asked, 'May I be excused?' and then I left without waiting for a reply.

"In my room, I went back to working on my current project, soldering components onto the circuit board of a build-it-yourself Heathkit shortwave radio receiver. It never did work. Just smoked and smelled awful when I turned it on for the first time. A week later I threw it out."

I realized that I had used my real name in the story. I watched her closely as I said, "Not very dramatic, I know. Grim fairy tales."

Sally's smile came back on and her eyes sparkled, lighting up the whole room. "Yeah, Warren, we've both been knocked around. Thanks for playing full out with me. No more stories. Now come over here and kiss me."

Necking took a little choreography with someone in a wheelchair. She directed the scene change and I took orders. Soon we had our seats next to each other, so that her chair faced front and mine faced toward back. This was a makeshift love couch. We could lean over on our armrests and neck in comfort.

Our first kiss began gentle but not tentative. We went slowly, brushing our lips against each other. We both wanted to stretch out the tension. As our mouths barely touched, the lightness of the caress of her lips on mine became excruciating, yet I hung there, relishing the smell of wine on her breath, the softness of her lips, and the slowness of our lovemaking. She made a soft moaning sound and then I felt the wet, urgent warmth of her tongue in my mouth.

I think I might have let out a tiny cry, too. I felt my erection and the familiar insistent desire to be inside this woman. But there was something a little scary emerging in my loins. A yielding. I realized with surprise that I also wanted her to take me.

With no warning she wheeled backward and broke our contact. Her pupils were wide, and she was out of breath. I could see her nipples erect under the silken fabric of her dress. She said, "I'm not a prick tease but I like to go slowly. Don't expect to fuck me anytime soon. I'm very careful."

I smiled and my voice was warm and husky when I said, "Shut up and come back here."

She wheeled toward me. I reached out and stroked the side of her cheek with the edge of my index finger. I brushed my finger across her mouth, and her lips opened.

Then I felt her retreat a little. Something in her eyes drew back. I said, "Look, Sally, you're totally in charge. We move at your pace. I just wanted to touch you."

She rekindled that smile. "I want to touch you, too. Everywhere. But now I want you to go. This is a perfect moment, right at the beginning, when everything is humming with tension and anticipation. I want to hoard it for a while."

I was put off. My animal soul inside doesn't really understand delayed gratification. The wolf wanted to mate. But I was old enough not to be led around by my penis any longer. Barely. So I compromised and asked, "When can we do this again?"

She teased me. "Closing for the sale, Warren? At heart you're always a Nordstrom clerk. How about next Wednesday night?"

Everybody wants to meet with me on my therapy night. I countered, "How about Tuesday?"

"Basketball for me. Thursday?"

"Done, we have a sale. Thanks for inviting me over. I want more."

"Me, too. Ripley, show the man out." She pointed her hand at me and said in a high soprano tone, *"Spelen!"*

Ripley jumped up and lunged for me. Before I could move she had me pinned to my chair and was ferociously licking my face. "Help!" I cried while Sally hooted.

Finally she said, "Okay, Ripley. *Zit!"*

Ripley jumped off and moved next to Sally's chair, where she sat quietly. Sally was still giggling as I stood up and brushed off black dog hair. She said, "I just taught her that. Aggressive affection. This is the first time I've tried it on someone else. It works great. Canine tongue attack techniques."

I said, "I like your tongue better."

"Well, I'm glad of that."

I wasn't through. "Strindberg hated dog owners. He said they were cowards who didn't have the guts to bite people themselves."

Sally laughed, then bit down on air and said, "Come on over and try me."

"Maybe Thursday," I said. I could prick-tease a little, too. I walked outside.

The stars were out. On the way to my car, I watched them flicker between the tree branches. Okay, maybe they weren't looking down on me. But if they were, they'd be jealous.

CHAPTER TWENTY-FIVE

I t was Saturday and I was back on the Ave, selling dreams. I love this street. It's the heart of Berkeley. East Coasters like to sneer about how the continent tilted and all the nuts rolled over to California. Damn straight.

Berkeley is the only city in the United States that has a foreign policy. Sure, we still have one sandaled foot permanently stuck in the sixties. But, as open to ridicule as this city is, Berkeley still manages to remind the rest of the nation that once there was a time when love was free, when youth felt like they could change the world, and then they did.

Today the dreamers of the sixties are anesthetized in the pursuit of new toys, better entertainment, stronger drugs, and retirement. The totalitarian empire reigns while its citizens snooze. Visions of social justice have transformed into fantasies of new Hummers and Disney World vacations. But someday the sleepers will awake. One morning the now-docile prisoners will look around and recognize their bars and chains. Revolution will return. And I bet it's going to start right here, on Telegraph Avenue.

But not on this day. The vendors squeezed the pedestrians to the wall, slowing foot traffic enough to inspire impulse buying. It was show time for capitalism on this retro Main Street where the leftovers from the summer of love mix with tribal piercing grunge.

My first customer didn't fit the picture of someone who would dream of using my New Age services. He was a teenage pseudo gangster: blue rag on his head, T-shirt that announced, "Beer Is My Copilot," baggy blue jeans, and $300 Nike Air Jordan basketball shoes. He didn't even want a reading. He just asked for one of my cards, said it was for his mother. I gave him one and he walked off. I didn't think too much about it at the time.

After him, I hit the zone. This must be what its like when a gambler gets on a roll: the ball falls in double zero, the dice come up seven, and your hole card is an ace. I picked up that my first customer was on his way to see his mistress by noticing the white band of skin on his ring finger. I caught on that client number two, a Cal student, was on her way to flunking out when I smelled last night's alcohol underneath the mouthwash she was using. Customer number three was floored that I knew that she had just lost her job. That one came entirely out of the blue.

When you're hot, you're hot, and I was cookin'. Or, as Sally would put it, "You were attuned to the chaoritic conditions and anticipating the directionality of the unfolding patterns." And then some!

All the attunement in the world wouldn't prepare me for my next client. She had a dark complexion, brown eyes, hair turning from brown to gray cut in a long pageboy, jeans, and a cheap, imported white cotton blouse with flowers embroidered on it. I couldn't quite pin down her nationality—Indian, Central American, Portuguese? One of those totally normal, in-between people whom you forget five minutes after they leave.

She leaned forward and spoke softly in unaccented English, "I work for Max. Lay out the cards and pretend you are doing a reading for me." Then she leaned back and crossed her arms.

I laid out four cards in a diamond. Pointing to each one in turn I said, "So, what's up? I didn't expect direct contact. You must have something. Is anything wrong?"

Just then a pedestrian walked closer to my table so I said, "Major Arcana, wands and cups, Queen of the May, blah, blah, blah." The coast was again clear. "Speak."

She looked at me for a moment. Then she bent over the cards, appearing to examine them closely. She said, "Our surveillance on Hal Russell has turned interesting. He keeps going out to a run-down warehouse in Clayton."

She shook her head as if saddened by the spread in front of her. Then she said, "You've got two choices: Door number one, put surveillance on the building. Door number two, go out there tomorrow night and find out for yourself what's going on. If you want to do the second option, our people will pick the outside locks and watch the perimeter. The breaking and entering is your job. That little adventure will cost you an additional five hundred dollars."

I laid a card in the middle of the diamond and said, "Okay, I want door two. Any chance we can do it tonight?"

She shook her head, and wiped an imaginary tear from her eye. "No chance, manpower shortage. Sunday or nothing."

I nodded sympathetically and said, "Let's start at ten P.M. Where will I meet you?"

She reached over and touched the card, nodded, looked up at me, and then said, "the Diablo Associated Real Estate office on the corner of Ygnacio Valley and Clayton Road. We'll be in a U-Haul van. Bring the pager Max gave you." She took $20 out of her purse and handed it to me, stood up, and walked into the crowd.

Easiest twenty I ever made, even if it was my own money. I looked down at our bogus reading. There in the middle rested the card with no number, the Fool. I hoped it wasn't the universe making a nasty comment about my level of sagacity.

Right after she left, I reaffirmed my lack of psychic abilities. I should have been hit with a blast of premonition and left for home. But I just happily sat there completely unprepared for the next visitor. My messenger had no sooner faded into anonymity than I spied a familiar, unwelcome figure, aimed at my table like a cruise missile. Oh, lucky me, it was the FBI's finest, Special Agent Dave.

I waved at him and gestured for him to come over, as if that made a difference. When he got within earshot, I said, "Sit down, Dave. I'll give you a complimentary reading. I just sensed you were going to run into me today."

He stood over me. "Cut the clairvoyant shit, Ritter. I have some questions for you. I need you to come down to the FBI Field Office in the city at 450 Golden Gate Avenue, on the thirteenth floor. I need to see you there this afternoon, or Monday afternoon."

"That won't work for me," I replied coolly. "But I seem to have spare time right now. Pull up the chair, Dave, and sit down in *my* office, unless you have a warrant to arrest me."

His cheeks were red with tiny white spots. A Christmas effect. I didn't think it was a sign of happiness. He grabbed the chair and sat down with a hard thud. Every cent I spent on that steel-reinforced, extra-heavy-duty frame was paying off now.

He said, "If you don't want privacy, it's fine by me." It obviously wasn't. "You worked at Nordstrom from 1996 until 1998, correct?"

"Yep." I'd keep my answers as short as possible.

"Did you ever work in men's furnishings?"

"Sure."

"Was there a lot of theft in those departments?"

"I don't know. I didn't work security."

"How easy would it be to steal, oh, say, a pair of shoes from the floor?"

"I don't know. I didn't work security."

"But you must have some sense of how easy or difficult that might have been."

"Nope." That was the windup, here comes the pitch.

He leaned forward. "Well, you *would* know how easy it might be for a shop clerk to walk off with a nice pair of shoes."

"Nope. I don't know if I told you this, but I didn't work in security. Mostly I sold overpriced dresses to overweight housewives who wanted to look anorexic. I can't help you with your shoplifting investigation."

I was really pissing him off. He got up and said, "Well, Mr. Ritter, I can see you are being obstinate. Perhaps I better go and obtain that warrant and see if that might make you a little more manageable."

Oh, goodie, threats. My tax dollars at work. "If that's what you need to do. I have just one piece of advice. Let's consult the cards." I turned over the top card in the deck. It was the Nine of Swords. The card depicted a woman sobbing in her bed while nine sharp swords were mounted above her. I said, "This card tells me you're stuck in your investigation. The pressure to produce a kidnapper is rising and you have nothing. You're losing it. You wake up at three in the morning, covered with sweat."

He looked at the card and was still for a moment. His face paled. Then he shook his head and said, "Screw you, fortune-teller. I don't know what you're talking about. I do know you're guilty of something. And I'm going to find out what. You'd better get a lawyer!" With that brilliant exit line, he strode off.

Like I said, I was on a roll.

Then the tarot muse left me. I felt empty and foolish, wasting my life sitting on a street corner amusing pedestrians. An overweight guy in a corduroy jacket, turtleneck, and khakis sat down and wanted to know about his tenure. I laid out the cards, but they were just stupid pictures painted on cardboard. My subscription to the akashic records had been temporarily suspended. "I'm sorry, Professor, but I just got a raging headache. I can't continue right now. Here's your money back." I packed up for the day.

I stopped at the mailboxes and picked up my latest missive from Sally. That girl was producing! When I got back in my apartment, I turned the bookshelf toward the wall, converting the place into command central. If I didn't get this guy, I'd run out of pushpins soon.

Reading Sally's material or, more precisely, Detective Flemish's material, didn't make things any clearer. The statewide hunt for Louise's blue V70 Volvo station wagon had turned up zilch. Frank Wellington looked clean. Curtis had lied through his teeth to the cops.

Curtis Jackson hadn't been anywhere near the animal shelter the night Louise was murdered. Flemish had logged a call from Berkeley Homicide letting him know that Jackson was considered a primary suspect for the murder. Another animal shelter worker told an investigator that she had covered for Jackson that night. He had called her early, saying he was too sick to come in. His mother had already given a statement that he was at work that night. Trouble in Oak Town. Berkeley Homicide recommended continuing to look for evidence linking Jackson with Oakland gangs and with the kidnapping.

What was worse was an additional note Sally included. "I hacked into Curtis's e-mail account. AOL, no problem. Anyway, thought you might be interested in this little message, sent three days before Heather was grabbed." Attached was this e-mail:

```
Subj: Deep shit about my new sweetie
Date: 3/24/04 10:35 AM Pacific Standard Time
From: CJShaft@aol.com
To: Bullet3417@hotmail.com
Sent from the Internet (Details)


   Yo, Bullet:
   Hey, I just found out some real scoop about
Heather, my new fox. Her old lady is loaded.
We're talking mills here. Wouldn't it be sweet
if some of that flowed my way! Her stepdad's a
dick, but that's not the real prob. Mom hates
black folks. Sure would be nice if they both got
iced and my little H became a millionairess.
Dream on! Catch you tonight at Washington's.
Later. CJ
```

I would need to have a little chat with Mr. Curtis before the Man picked him up, which might be at any moment.

Then another complication. I'd love to pin the whole thing on Hal the ex-boyfriend. Since Berkeley was handling that I didn't have any information about his alibi for the murder night, but he was well alibied for the kidnapping. The guy I saw in the car with him told the police that, after hassling us, they went over to a bar on San Pablo, shot pool, and drank until the place closed at one. Unfortunately, the bartender remembered them, though not fondly. I angrily pinned up that sheet under "Hal Alibi." Of course, Hal didn't need to do it in person. One of his gang members might have done the job. Which helped me not at all.

Pretty soon I'll prove that no one did anything. The crimes were committed by rogue Klingons in a cloaked spacecraft.

I checked the time. If I jogged I could get to my dojo in time for the last Saturday class. I really needed to throw people around the room.

CHAPTER TWENTY-SIX

It never pays to do aikido with an attitude. It always back-fires. Time and again my anger drove me to attack, and I ended up flying through the air and landing hard. I just didn't have the patience to be present.

Limping home from the dojo, I got near Dwight when I felt an odd prickling down my back. I looked around but didn't see anything unusual. Still, it made me uneasy all the rest of the way home.

I crawled onto my European Sleepworks mattress after taking five Advil and hoped that a long night's sleep might make moving more comfortable. No luck. One-thirty in the morning and I was lying there wide awake, aching, and nervous as a cat in heat. I knew nothing was going to put me back asleep. I got up and silently screamed as my body reminded me of those falls. The only cure to my electric aches was to move, so I got on my jogging clothes and set off across Berkeley.

I love running during the graveyard shift. The city is almost silent. No one else stirs. The steam from the giant generators under the university breathes moist smoke from vents in the ground. Running through those clouds of steam is like moving through the breath of Earth. Passing an occasional streetlight, you travel across an island of amber in the vast black sea of the night.

But tonight was different. I couldn't relax. That same itchy feeling that accompanied me on my trip home from the dojo remained. I came out of the campus through Sather Gate and headed on to Telegraph. An occasional mound of clothing shuddered as I ran past a homeless person, but otherwise the well-lit sidewalks were empty.

Almost empty. I heard footfalls matching mine, coming from behind. I slowed down. Just like in the slasher films, the footsteps slowed. I spun around and spotted a man in the distance. He stopped and said something into his cell phone. This didn't look good.

I could hear cars coming from all directions. A lowrider entered Bancroft and blocked off the entrance to the university. Another one, a block up Telegraph, just turned on its lights. I could see two beaters turning toward the Ave to my right and my left.

If I ran hard, I might be able to break out of this net. If they didn't shoot me first, and if I didn't run right into them in the dark. Whoever this was would box me in sooner or later. I might as well get this thing over with. At least I couldn't be much more bruised than I already was.

The guy with the cell came closer. He was wearing a black T-shirt with the sleeves ripped off and black Levi's. The shirt had an orange radiation emblem on it and the word "BIO-HAZARD." He sported a long tattoo of a snake wrapped around his right arm. Unfortunately, his face was familiar. The last time I saw this gentleman he was giving me the finger. It was Hal, Heather's ex-boyfriend.

Where were cops when you needed them? Here I was, on one of Berkeley's main streets, the only moving vehicles in the whole town surrounding me. Five hulks were getting out of them to kick my ass. Where were the guys driving the cars that have "Protecting and Serving our Community" written all over them? The boys in navy blue were all hanging out at Top Dog drinking coffee and shooting the shit while I get pounded.

Hal moved in. I thought I'd try taking the offensive. "Excuse me, do I know you?" I asked.

"You sure as hell do, Mr. Fortune-Teller. You know me well enough to give the police my address and phone number." Oh, shit!

He went on, "The cop who interrogated me gave me your name as the informant. I don't know how the hell you got that information. My phone's unlisted. But I'm going to make sure that you regret passing it along. You sure as shit ain't going to be passing along anything else for a while."

By now I was in a close circle of thugs. Three of them were Hispanic, the other two white. They were all big. I could do some fancy aikido. Throw a couple of them onto the concrete sidewalk and really make them mad. No, that worked only in *Matrix*. Here it could get me killed.

The nice thing about a hopeless situation is that it can't get worse. Any improvisation might improve things. Whatever I tried, when it failed, then I'd get beat up. That was going to happen anyway.

I didn't hesitate. I began ranting, "That goddamn motherfucker. Flemish said he was going to fuck me, and he did. Fuckin' pigs, if they can't beat the crap out of you, they set up somebody else to do the job. Assholes!" I spread my arms wide. They were looking at me like I was psycho. "Sure, go ahead, guys, take your best shot. You won't have to worry about me turning you in. The Man set you on me in the first place. You're covered, so beat the crap out of me."

At least that stopped the pack from coming any closer. Hal said, "What the fuck are you talkin' about?"

Talk loud, talk fast, stall for time. A meteor might hit Earth right in front of me. Once the thumping starts there is no more opportunity. I said, "Look, I got a Danville homicide lieutenant, name of Flemish, pissed off at me. I set him up to catch a lot of shit from his commanding officer. He warned me he was going to find a way to pay me back. And here you are.

"I mean, think about it, Hal, how often does a cop tell you the name of his informant? Has it ever happened to you?" I looked around at the other wolves. "Or to anybody else you know? Hell no!"

I slumped my shoulders in defeat. "He knew you'd kick my ass. Hey, if I ratted you out I'd deserve to get my ass whipped." I looked up at Hal. Here comes the big pitch. "But Hal, I mean, it don't even make sense. How the hell would I get your unlisted number, from a crystal ball? Be real, I can barely pay my own phone bill." Long speech. I put my bet on the table. Let's see if the bluff worked.

Hal stood there. His eyes were shining in the lamplight. He didn't look stupid. Was that in my favor or against me?

Finally he spoke, slowly and distinctly. "I have other uses for you. I don't need to take you out, yet. But if I *ever* find out that you ran a con on me, I will not come back and beat you up. I will come and kill you. Do you understand that, tarot boy?"

Boy? I was more than twice his age. Not a good time to

point that out, though. I kept it simple and subservient. "Yes, I understand, Hal."

He turned around and started walking toward a car at the end of the street. The circle broke up. I stood still until I heard the last car drive off. I started back toward home, my legs trembling. I really needed to take a leak.

After making a pit stop, I called up Flemish. I got his voice mail. I unloaded. "What the hell is going on in your hick town, Flemish? This is Warren Ritter, and I just got back from almost getting the shit kicked out of me by a gang of Concord hoods. Do you want to know *why* they were coming after me? I'd be glad to tell you. One of your frigging rookie cops told Hal from hell that I'd fingered him. What kind of stupid police work is that? Are you trying to get me killed? Because you did a damn good job of it tonight! If they had broken my legs, I'd have sued your lamebrain department for two million dollars. Call me and tell me exactly what you're up to." I enjoyed slamming that handset into its cradle. The advantage of heavy old telephones.

CHAPTER TWENTY-SEVEN

I slept about three hours. I kept waking up and replaying that scene with Hal's rat pack, with increasingly disastrous endings. I woke up to the morning shaken but at least not broken.

Those guys scared me. If they had killed Louise, I was going to see they stayed in jail for the rest of their lives. If they were innocent of that crime, I was going to avoid them like anthrax. Tonight I'd find out. I cleaned the place up and got ready for my workday.

Back on the Ave, I found it difficult to keep my mind focused on prophecy. I kept thinking about how stupid I was to be planning to break into the lair of the same mad dogs who'd threatened to kill me last night. A *very* stupid plan, but then sometimes I'm a very stupid guy.

At 12:45 a surprise visitor showed up. Frank Wellington was casually dressed in crisply creased navy slacks and a gray short-sleeved oxford shirt. But he had dark shadows under his gray eyes, eyes that had just looked upon the swamp in the fifth ring of Hades. He politely asked if he could have a moment with me. I gestured to the client chair and he sat down gratefully.

"I'm here to apologize," he said. It didn't look like he had a lot of practice at making amends. The words came out slowly. "I was rude to you in my office. I was expecting a ransom call. It didn't come until the next day. Anyway, we still don't have Heather back. The FBI has done nothing but get in the way. I made a mistake calling them in." He shook his head, like he just realized that he had wandered off of his main track. Too bad, I could listen all day to someone trashing the feds. Then he finished, lamely, "I just wanted to say I'm sorry."

I could be charitable, especially when I was the one who had been so obnoxious. "I understand. It was my fault. I should not have been bothering you at that time. The pressure you're under must be enormous."

He looked at me, the whites of his eyes contrasting with the dark bags beneath. "I'm afraid I threw you out before finding out why you wanted to speak with me. You said on the phone that Louise had told you something. What was it?"

My energized mind spun in a sizzling circle and came up with nothing. I decided stupidity might be the best course, "Gosh, Mr. Wellington, that was a while ago. I can't really remember. For the life of me I can't recall what it was. I'm sorry. It must not have been too important."

He sighed. Relief, exhaustion, I couldn't tell which. I said, "Look, I know you don't like this tarot hocus-pocus, but I'd like to give you one of my cards, in case you need to contact me in the future. I'm sorry, but I use tarot cards as my business cards." I grabbed a card from the deck and pasted my label on it, the King of Wands: a red-haired monarch sat on his flaming throne looking out over his desert kingdom. "Ah," I said, "the card of a dynamic, imaginative, and forceful leader."

Frank began to look annoyed, but he marshaled what self-management skills he had left. He said, "Thank you," and took the card. Another one had stuck to the bottom, and it slipped out of his grasp and onto the table: the Eight of Swords. I said nothing.

He thanked me and left. I watched a few minutes later as a silver Lexus with an American flag on the personalized license plate WELNGTN drove past. Frank didn't even glance at me. I no longer existed to Mr. Wellington.

The Eight of Swords sat there looking back at me. That card kept haunting me. It still had a role to play in this drama. I could catch only a glimmer of what that might be.

Frank had seemed sincere. I wish I trusted my fellow man more. But I didn't. I wished I was a lot more psychic. But I wasn't. I kept seeing Heather stuffed into a garbage bag as I sorted through my bag of tarot cards to find replacements.

A vast shadow fell upon my table. I looked up, expecting to see an eclipse. Instead, acres of a linen suit blotted out the Ave. It took a while to see around the bulk and make it all the way up past the rippling mass of chins to those bottomless brown eyes.

I remembered that low voice well, even though it had been decades since Mexico. He said, "The bruises healed up pretty good."

I stood up, not that it mattered that much. He was a good-sized hill of flesh. Bending my neck to look at him, I held out my hand and said, "Philip?"

One huge, simian hand engulfed mine and gave it a tender shake.

"We were not properly introduced the last time we met. I am Philip Letour. I was not expecting to see you ever again after that rather short reading."

"Hello, Philip. I don't think I ever told you my name back in Mexico. I'm Warren Ritter. I stayed away from your side of the city after that night. You scared the shit out of me. And now, look at me, here I am, a protégé."

"No surprise there. Darkness and light wove around each other in that reading. Too bad you didn't hang around long enough to see it unfold. It started with tragedy and ended up with the Magician Card mating with the High Priestess—the cards chose you that night. From then on, it was only a matter of *when* they would come to claim you."

He made no gesture to sit on my steel chair, thank goodness. It wouldn't have survived. He moved around the table until he was opposite me. The foot traffic moved away from our table, as though pedestrians were magnetically repelled by this behemoth. Philip sighed. "You're in trouble. I don't need cards to read that: it's written in the twisted lines around your eyes. Do you need my help?"

I'd lived a lifetime avoiding those Samaritans who want to try to help me. Help turns sour in an instant, and then I need to get out of town. I help myself. That's the only way it can work. So I was shocked at what came out of my mouth.

"Yes."

He reached inside his linen jacket and pulled out those ancient cards of his. I remembered those hands, unlike any that I had ever seen. The lines in his hands were deep trenches. His fingers were long and thick. These were hands that might be able to crush coal into diamonds. Some atavistic recessive gene came forward in utero to give him hands for swinging on branches rather than for dealing tarot cards. He gently set his deck upon my table and said, "I never let anyone touch my cards. But today is an exception. Cut the deck four times."

I carefully reached over to pick up a section of the deck. An odd, almost nauseous feeling came up in me as my fingers made contact. There was big mojo here. I made four piles and was relieved not to have to touch those cards anymore. There was heavy-duty energy on that table. I was not in Philip's league.

Philip turned over each pile so that four cards were exposed: the Four of Coins, Justice, the Three of Hearts, and High Priestess. He was silent for a long time. Finally he said, "Greed, Warren. Greed lies at the heart of the darkness that is reaching out to you. Find the source of that greed and you have whom you seek. And you must seek him. No one else can bring him to the judgment he deserves. Once you mete out that justice, your road branches. Choosing one path leads you to freedom, but at the price of great suffering for three who love you. Along the other, steeper path awaits your anima. I don't think you are yet ready for that climb."

I didn't understand him very well. It sounded like he was encouraging me to continue my investigation, but the junk about suffering and anima was Greek to me. He swept up the cards before I could say anything and they disappeared into his jacket. Then he said, "The choices you imagine that you have are highly illusory. Almost every step of your life is an inevitable outcome of the steps you took before. But you made a choice decades ago. The Tower card that you so hated in Mexico expressed the consequence of that choice. Another moment of decision is fast approaching. Who you will become for the next thirty years will be decided by what you do in that moment." He handed me a business card with only an e-mail address on it:

PhilipLetour@aol.com. "This is for when you need me. Good-bye, Warren."

I said, "Good-bye, Philip," to the vast expanse of his back. He had already turned and was heading east, parting the tide of pedestrians in his wake.

I kept working for a couple more hours. A part of me did my job; I reassured or warned my clients. But the most alive part of me was getting ready to check out that warehouse. Would I get busted? Would I get killed? Would I find Heather, or her corpse? Would I run away? That was the most shameful of the scenes that my mind spun out.

Toward the afternoon, a dry wind kicked up. The southeast wind, coming over from the central valley. In summer we called it the firestorm wind because it took out most of the Berkeley hills in '91. It makes everybody edgy. It was too windy to read cards unless I wanted them blown down to the waterfront.

As I was packing up my table, I noticed that one of my cards had fallen into the gutter. A car had run over it. When I looked closer I saw that it was the King of Wands with my label on it. Frank had tossed it. Oh, well, I guess that card wasn't going to end up on his altar.

I finished putting my stuff away in the back room of the bookstore. I ate dinner. All the while I was busy imagining my upcoming adventure. I dressed in black. I could drive out to Antioch and get one of my guns. I liked the idea of going mano a mano against Hal, pistols blazing.

However, occasionally even I have a touch of common sense. *Ritter,* I asked myself, *what should happen in the unlikely event that you get caught by the police? If you are unarmed, they book you for a simple breaking and entering, you post bail, and then disappear. But if you're armed, you have the B and E plus carrying a concealed weapon, and bail becomes a bit more problematical. Plus you lose your expensive Kimber .45 when you disappear. Finally, should you be successful in ridding the world of Hal Russell, bail may be completely out of the picture. They might just lock you up forever.* So instead of a gun, I grabbed the book I was reading. Then I was off and away.

The Hispanic lady who set this meet up got out of a U-Haul in the empty parking lot and started right in, no greeting. "Number one, this meeting and the one we had earlier never happened. If I were to ask you to commit perjury, that would be encouraging you to break the law and Max would lose his license. So I won't do that." She paused.

I said, "This meeting never happened and I've never seen you in my life. I'd swear to that on a stack of Bibles."

"Good," she said. I'd passed the first test.

"Got your pager?" she asked.

I pulled it out to show her.

"Put it on vibrate," she ordered. "Now, here's how tonight is going down. Remember this story! You asked us to put this warehouse under surveillance, which we are doing. You instructed us to page you if anything unusual happened. Which we will. Then you decided *on your own* to commit the crime of breaking and entering, which we knew nothing about.

"We saw someone drive up to the building late at night but didn't recognize you. Since this was an unusual occurrence, we paged you. If someone ever checks the cell records, that call will establish that we were just doing our job. You went to the door at the rear of the warehouse and, remarkably enough, you found it unlocked, another event that we had nothing to do with. You entered the building.

"Then one of two things happened. Scenario A: you later exited the building and drove home, and we continued surveillance for the rest of the night. Scenario B: someone drove up while you were in the building. At that point we paged you again and then decided that we were in danger of discovery with so many people around. So we broke off the surveillance for the night and drove away.

"There is no scenario where we come in like the cavalry to help you out. Once you walk through that door, you are on your own. Do you understand that?"

I nodded.

She looked me up and down. There was a skeptical look on her face. She asked, "Do you have a flashlight?"

Oops. I was really a nouveau burglar. "Nope."

"Buy one. All right. It is now ten-thirteen. Go to a bar and make sure you are remembered there. Leave there so that you show up at the warehouse at 213 Summer Street at midnight. Don't come early, or that door might be locked. Do you understand?"

"Yes. I'll see you then."

"No, you won't." She got back in the van and drove off.

CHAPTER TWENTY-EIGHT

Clayton was, for the most part, a failed attempt to copy Orinda. It had a quaint downtown about two blocks long, lined with Victorian houses. Surrounding it were vast developments with attached golf courses and cookie-cutter houses on one-eighth-of-an-acre lawns. Except for downtown and a couple of scattered ranches, everything had been built in the past twenty years. The trees along the streets were skinny and in their adolescence.

Clayton was where the second vice presidents lived, the ones who lacked the drive to get any farther up the ladder. They were content with being comfortably upper middle class.

There was a run-down transition zone on the border of Clayton and Concord. The targeted warehouse lay in this area. Go a block farther, and you were in Concord, which was just like being in any other depressed industrial city.

I drove to the 7-Eleven and bought a flashlight, batteries, and a pair of gloves. Wasn't I the clever one! Then I headed toward Concord and stopped at the first bar I found, the Hot Spot.

It wasn't. Just a dive where alcoholics could hang out on the way down. Working-class guys were hiding out, avoiding the old lady and the whiny brats. Divorced guys were trying to get laid in hopes of forgetting what they screwed up. Women addicted to love, drugs, booze, or hunger were trolling for dreams. Just another bar.

I walked up to the rail and ordered a lemonade. The bartender just stared at me for a moment while my message slowly registered. Then he said, "You've got to be kidding."

"How about sarsaparilla?" I asked.

"Hey, buddy, this ain't the Comedy Channel. Order a real drink or get out."

Well, at least he'd remember me. "Any nonalcoholic beer?"

He sighed. "Yeah, I think I got some in the back."

One last shot at notoriety. "Any on tap?"

"Right." He rummaged around in the back of the cooler, came up with a Sharp's, and slammed it down in front of me. Obviously teetotaling was not a commonly accepted virtue in this milieu.

I put on my reading glasses, pulled out *The Fall of Berlin,* and started to read, which was rather challenging in the lousy light. I stretched three bottles of Sharp's for an hour and a half. Finally, it was time to go. I left a twenty on the bar, just to make another lasting impression, and got back in my car.

Summer Street was a lane of cracked pavement off Clayton Road. The warehouse was set well back from the curb, tucked next to a building with a sign in chipped paint that read "Diablo Ductwork Supply House." On the other side, a fenced-in lot was filled with gutted trucks. I didn't see Max's people anywhere.

One bare spotlight lit the empty parking lot in front of the one-story metal building. I parked in the shadow of the Duct-

176

work building and checked my watch: 12:03. Then I boldly walked up to the building and along the walkway that went along the left side. Near the end of this sidewalk was a sturdy metal door. Just beyond the door a chain-link fence blocked off the back of the building. This was a one-way passage.

My pager vibrated in my pocket, just like my señorita had promised. I put on my gloves and pulled out my flashlight. Sure enough, that door was unlocked. They came through for me. Here goes!

Darkness. Thick and complete. There were windows in the front of the building, so I didn't dare turn on the lights. I closed the door behind me but not enough to latch it, since I might be flying out of there at top speed. I switched on my light.

I could hear his claws on the concrete floor before I saw anything. He was coming top speed, moving too fast to bark. Damn, I wished I had that gun! I had no weapon. He was well armed, with a mouthful of daggers. I had to do something.

If he had been Ripley, sent on command by his master, I would be torn up if not killed. But he was a guard dog, trained to attack intruders but not under a command to take me out specifically. That gave him choices. Dogs are not good with choices.

I pointed the light up on my face, bared my teeth, and ran toward the oncoming dog, growling and barking fiercely. If I had been another dog, I would have ended up a pile of kibble. But this guy had never seen a human acting like a dog before. He was confused. Fang skidded to a stop as I waved my arms and jumped up and down barking away. Trying to figure out this strange turn of events, the bulky German shepherd cocked his head to one side.

Then I fell on the floor, rolled over, exposed my neck to the dog, and began whining piteously. He came over and sniffed me. I kept my arms and legs up in the air, arched my neck so that he had an even clearer shot at ripping out my larynx. I whimpered.

He snuffed again. Then he raised one leg and peed on me, a gesture of complete contempt. He was top dog. I whimpered again, and he walked over to his bed and lay down. I slowly got up and began walking around. He paid me no further attention. I was a wimp, no threat to him or his territory.

I resolved someday to write Bruce Fogle a letter of thanks for his book *The Dog's Mind*. He taught me this piece of canine behavior. One side of my body stank of dog urine, but it was a small price to pay. Better that than blood. I began inspecting my surroundings.

I was in a huge open room filled with cars—Toyota Camrys, Honda Accords, Chevy Caprices, a smattering of Lexuses, BMWs, and an occasional SUV. Some of the cars were in states of deconstruction. Others looked new. At first I thought auto repair, but as I looked closer I realized that this shop was exactly the opposite. The cars were being dismantled. This was a chop shop, where stolen cars were torn apart for parts.

I shined my light around. No little rooms where teenagers might be handcuffed. Just one big space filled with cars, tools strewn around the floor, and piles of car parts. The only doors were the one in front and the one I came through. The front windows were boarded over from the inside so that no one could look in. I inspected the one other room, a tiny bathroom, empty and disgusting. This was a bust.

I was turning to go when I saw a flicker of blue. I shined my light in that direction and saw a blue Volvo V70 station wagon. The wheels were off, the engine was out, the side windows were missing, as was the front seat. I walked over and shined my light inside. The glove compartment door hung open. Nothing inside. On a hunch I reached in where the passenger window had been removed and pulled down the passenger-side sun visor.

There, strapped on the back of the visor, was a leather organizer with a registration card showing behind a plastic window. I peered closer. Sure enough, the Volvo was registered to Frank Wellington. I put the visor back up and turned toward the rear door. That's when the vibrator went off in my pocket. My spotters were letting me know someone was on his way in.

If I ran out the back door, I would be detected the minute I hit the perimeter of the spotlight. There was no way I was going over the back fence, which had razor wire on the top. Exiting the building was a losing proposition.

When I heard a key in the front door, I turned off my flashlight, dropped down on the concrete, and rolled under a Mercedes. Harsh lights came on, brilliantly illuminating the shop. I heard voices, one with a thick Spanish accent and the other a voice I had last heard telling me that if I conned him he'd kill me. It was my old friend Hal Russell.

The other guy spoke a harsh command in Spanish to the dog, who had been growling from the moment he heard the key in the lock. The dog became silent and sat on his bed, watching the two carefully.

Hal said, "Yeah, Chops, shut up. God, I hate that barking. And it stinks in here. Fuckin' dog is pissing on everything." Hal was smelling my shirt.

Hal went on, "So Juan, what the fuck's going on here? Fuckin' silent alarm wakes me up out of a wet dream. It's not supposed to be set off by the dog."

The two of them began walking the perimeter of the room, Juan silent and Hal muttering. Soon I couldn't make out what he was saying. That is until Hal slammed the rear door and started cursing again, "Fuckin' Roy, *el stupido,* he was supposed to lock up tonight. Christ, do I have to wet-nurse every one of those bastards? The fuckin' door's wide open. The wind must have blown it. Shit, we could have lost Chops. I'm going to bust Roy one!"

There was a mumbled reply from Juan. Hal said, "Let's get the hell out of here. I don't need this crap. There is too much shit going down right now as it is. This fucking shop is the least of my worries. Chops is all the alarm we need. He'll rip anybody's balls off that wanders in here." The two of them left through the front door.

I sighed in relief. Chops was relieved, too. I rolled out from under the car and brushed myself off. He growled at me once and then lay back down on his bed.

I looked out the front window just in time to see Hal and Juan driving off in a white van. Shit, does everybody in this case drive a freakin' white van? I waited for half an hour, just long enough for Hal to get back home and settle down. Then I opened the front door and walked out, imagining the alarm ringing in his bedroom. I left the door open in case Chops wanted a new life, got in my car, and drove a few blocks away. I checked my watch, pulled out my cell phone, and called the Danville police.

I used a phony French accent, "I haf zom information for vous. Ze car you are seeking, ze bleu Volvo station wagon zat vas driven by ze Wellington woman, is rrright now at 213 Summer Street, off of Clayton Road, in ze how-you-say transition of Clayton and Concord. Ze automobile thief will be there in just a few minutes. Zut alors—hurry, and you may entrap him. Au revoir."

I drove off, wishing the very worst for Monsieur RRRRussell.

CHAPTER TWENTY-NINE

I was nursing my latte the next morning, trying to get over yet another nightmare about climbing the red steps to nowhere, when what to my wondering eyes should appear but Special Agent Dave.

"I thought you frequented the café on Euclid?" he said as he sat down uninvited.

I was done with playing nice. "I'm slumming it. What brings you out crawling into the sunlight this morning?"

"What do you know about a chop shop in Concord that specializes in taking apart cars that owners want 'stolen' because they're tired of making car payments?"

"Sounds very enterprising, but not my line of work."

"You're a real wiseacre, aren't you? Last night somebody just fucked up a three-month undercover investigation of that place. You don't happen to know who that person was, do you?"

"Not a clue."

"Do you know French?" he asked.

It was an old line, but I just couldn't resist. "No, but if you hum a few notes . . ."

The guy had no sense of humor. "Knock it off. Do you speak French?"

"No, I hate the French. Ever since they refused to join us in Iraq, I have been reduced to 'Freedom' kissing my girlfriends, which isn't half so fun. It's hard to kiss and salute the American flag all at the same time."

I think Dave was getting tired of me and my wit. "Well, I just want you to know that I hope to have a warrant for your arrest by the end of the day. Then you can tell your un-American jokes to all the friendly boys locked up in the Alameda Detention Facility."

Having fired the final round, he got up and started to leave. Suddenly he spun around looking startled and pointed out the window toward something behind me and cried out, "Attendez!"

One of the oldest tricks in the book. Almost as hoary as, "There's a deputy behind you with a gun." I just looked at him and paraphrased in my best De Niro accent, "You talkin' to me? Who you talkin' to?"

He glared, spun around, and walked out.

My repartee had been clever, but still I was pretty worried about what he had told me. How much did they have against me? Were they looking for a judge's signature on that warrant right now, or was that just blowing smoke? I shivered.

I knew in my bones that I didn't have much time left. The coffee didn't take away my chill.

My cell phone went off. What next? I pushed a button. "Ritter here."

"Warren, I'm calling to apologize." It was Detective Flemish. I knew his voice quite well by now.

"Then apologize, by all means."

He took a deep breath. "Hal Russell was telling you the truth. We have a rookie cop who spends more time watching reality TV than listening in the police academy. I told him to contact the two Contra Costa–based suspects and arrange for them to come in for another interview with me. So he decides to embellish the invitation. He tells them that we have a new informant, a Berkeley psychic who's broken the case. He names you. He thought that would make them more nervous, and one of them would crack. He's been reassigned to parking violations indefinitely. I'm sorry. We owe you one."

Owed by a cop. That *was* a first. I chose to be magnanimous. "Thanks for letting me know, Detective. I'm sure, by the time this whole thing has ended, we'll be even-steven. So long." I clicked off.

That call was a refreshing contrast to the previous encounter, but I still felt uneasy. I didn't know what to do to get rid of a growing dread that things were beginning to unravel. Well, panic wasn't going to help anyone. It really didn't matter what I did, as long as I did something.

"Something" looked like grabbing a latte to go and heading back up to my apartment. I pulled a chair in front of the mass of cards, papers, Post-it notes, and drawings plastered all over the back of my bookcase. I sat and unfocused my eyes a little and let my gaze wander around the montage of data and images, looking for lines of connection.

I could see three threatening vectors that ended with Heather's kidnapping. Menace could originate from many directions and end up in her corner of the board. The anomaly was the murder of her mother. Which corner of the board did that threat originate from? Was it intentional, or an inadvertent by-product of the kidnapping? I thought about what Philip had told me. Where was the greed? Was it the Concord gang lord getting revenge, the con-man boyfriend working for the big score, or the stepdad who needed to be a widower?

My eyes kept returning to the tarot card of the Hanged Man pinned in the center of the paper maelstrom. The track to the solution led right through him. What if I was looking at this whole thing upside down? Maybe I was asking exactly the wrong questions. A pattern glimmered for a moment.

I called Sally on my cell. This time I got a message center. A neutral voice said, "The party you wish to reach is unavailable. You have one minute to leave a message."

Okay, here goes. "Nightrider here. Four items: Any hope for an autopsy? Who called the police to pin it on me? I need to know who inherits or financially benefits from the deceased's elimination. Financials on the boyfriend, the ex, and the old man. Thanks! Bye."

Fifteen seconds. Not bad.

I still had a couple of hours free this morning. Perhaps it was time to visit the lying boyfriend, Curtis. I still had the grease-stained shred of paper bearing Curtis Jackson's address and phone number in my wallet. I decided to surprise him and not call first. I was sure he loved surprises.

The Jackson residence was located near Mills College, one of the last all-women undergraduate programs in the country. College Heights consisted of two- to three-bedroom cute wooden houses in a nice neighborhood on the borderlands between predominately lower-class rough streets of downtown Oakland and the predominately upper-class homes in the hills. But as the housing prices continued to skyrocket, each year the area became more gentrified and bleached.

I walked up to a well-kept yellow-beige house with green

shutters and doors. Curtis's family looked like Oakland A's fans. The door was answered by a short, thin black woman with deep creases across her forehead. She was wearing a white tank top, running shorts, and Adidas cross trainers. A sheen of perspiration glistened on her face.

She spoke in a brisk, tight voice. "If you're a reporter, get the hell out of here. If you're a cop, show me some identification. Otherwise just leave us alone."

This had obviously been a rough month for the Jackson family. As she reached up to close the door I handed her the torn paper with Curtis's handwriting on it. "I'm neither of those things. But Curtis asked me to come by if I thought he needed help." A little lie here, but I had to keep that door open.

I immediately went on to say, "Look, if he doesn't want to see me, that's fine, I'll leave. But ask him first, please. Tell him it's the guy he spoke to at the Cheese Steak shop, the last guy to talk with Heather before she was kidnapped. Just ask. I think I can help him, if you'll let me." I struck a particularly sincere pose, arms open, eyes warm, voice low and caring. Come on, lady, it doesn't get more trustworthy than this!

She didn't look too impressed, but she said, "Wait here, I'll check it out," and closed the door. I'd won the first round.

Curtis opened the door looking like he came right off the mattress to greet me. He was dressed in a T-shirt and running pants that he probably just climbed into. "Hi," he said. "Sorry, I don't remember your name right now, but Mom said you wanted to see me."

"I'm Warren Ritter. Invite me in and I'll brew you a cup of coffee."

"Oh, Mom already made some. Sure, come on in." He yawned and led the way past a clean but lived-in living room and a dining room with a lovely cherrywood dining table, into a bright, spacious kitchen. From downstairs I heard the sounds of exercise machines being tortured. That woman knew how to work out!

He pointed me over to a corner of the kitchen with a built-in table and benches. "Black, sugar, cream?" he asked, a polite host even when mostly still asleep. "White and sweet," I replied. I sat down and looked at their rose garden in the backyard as he brought over two steaming mugs.

After a long gulp he looked at me and said, "Okay, what's up?"

I said, "I need to know about the night Louise Wellington got whacked."

He got instantly pissed, "Goddamn it. I'm sick of talking about that night, and I'm sick of being suspected of having anything to do with this. Look, if that's what you came over here to do, you can——"

"Easy!" I interrupted his tirade. I'd play good cop. "Look, Curtis, you're not the only one who's suspected of being a killer and kidnapper. I get daily visits from this asshole in the FBI who wants nothing better than to lock me up for keeps over this pile of poop. You and I are top contenders for the crime-of-the-month award. Just chill for a moment and remember I'm on your side, okay?"

Curtis took a long drink from his mug. Then he sighed. "Sorry. I'm just way too stressed about this. That Stiles prick has been threatening to bust me, too. I called that lawyer you gave me yesterday 'cause I was expecting to get picked up any minute."

"So look," I said, "we'll trade. I'll tell you where I was on that Sunday night and you show me yours. Deal?" I didn't wait for him to agree. "I was in bed asleep until Louise Wellington called me, around ten-thirty or eleven. Then I went back to sleep. How's that for a lame alibi?"

"Better than mine," he said. "I was so worried about Heather I couldn't stand it. I wasn't about to spend another night alone with a bunch of howling animals. I got a coworker to cover for me. Then I went out, bought a bottle of Wild Turkey and got shit-faced drunk, and passed out over at a friend's crib. Of course he was out of town, so no one can cover my sorry ass. Mom's ready to kill me. I feel like such a jerk, lying about it. I never really thought about alibis since I knew I didn't do it. Now I'm royally fucked."

"Hey," I said, trying to reassure him, "everybody lies to police. They're used to it. But it's a good thing you got a hold of Berkowitz. He's a great guy to have on your team in a full-court press. I've got to go. Thanks for the truth."

"No problem, and look out for your own self."

As I was leaving, Curtis's mother appeared at the top of the stairs, sweating. She said, "You bring Heather back here. She's a treasure. Her parents didn't deserve her. Keep her alive."

I had received my marching orders. I said, "Yes, ma'am, I'll do just that, ASAP."

As I drove away I mentally crossed Curtis off the suspect list, again. He might be a con artist, but there was no way he could kidnap or kill anyone. His petite mother would put him over her knee and whoop his butt if he ever tried something like that.

CHAPTER THIRTY

If Curtis was off the list, then it was time to see if I could put Hal back on it. I needed to bust his alibi for the day Heather got kidnapped. I headed for the Five Spot, a tiny dive on San Pablo. It was right out of the fifties: a pink neon cocktail glass in front of the place, a long bar along one side, and barely enough room for a couple of small round tables, a long maple shuffleboard table, and a coin-operated pool table in the back.

I pulled up a barstool and ordered a Bud. The bartender had a ferret head seated on shoulders that would make O.J. quake. His thick hands looked like they could crush the tall glass he plunked down in front of me. "You work Sunday nights, right?" I said. It was worth a shot.

"I work all the time. Why?" His voice was squeaky. He must have ferret vocal cords, too. Not that anyone was about to tease this flesh mountain.

"Oh, nothing. Just wondering if you remembered those loud-mouth little gangster punks that were in here a couple of Sundays ago."

His tiny, shiny eyes began to scan the room. Seeing that it was just the two of us, he locked back on me. "Who the fuck are you?"

"Hey, easy. I was just drinking here that night, and I think one of those bastards took my Zippo lighter. It belonged to my dad, and I'm trying to find it. Did anyone turn it in by any chance?"

"You're lying. Get the fuck out of my bar. Now, or I'll toss you out." He started for the end of the bar, but I was already out the door.

This was very interesting. Perhaps Mr. Ferrethead had perfect memory and had memorized every person who had come into his bar for the past month. But with a skull cavity that small, I doubted it. The only other way he could know that I was lying was if those punks hadn't been in the bar at all the night Louise was murdered. I wondered how much Hal had paid him for that alibi. I had more notes to write for the back of my bookcase.

CHAPTER THIRTY-ONE

Spring in Berkeley can turn cold and miserable. When the fog comes in, the wind gets chill and most natives pull out travel brochures for Baja. Worse, it can stay that way all summer. Hot, sunny days don't come until August and September.

But today, spring in Berkeley was just about perfect. This was one of the best days so far this year. Warm, friendly sunlight, cool breezes, clear sky, and roses blooming everywhere, a lovely day for a walk. I parked in a secret parking place that never gets ticketed behind an office building off Shattuck and headed up into the relatively car-free zone of the university. Once I walked away from the car, my body relaxed. I had been tense all morning for no known reason. But now I could breathe easier.

The entrance to the campus at Telegraph Avenue and Sproul Plaza is a squalid dump, littered with homeless panhandlers looking pathetic in hopes of catching the eye and purse of socially conscious underclassmen. Students strode past, much too caught up in their intense discussions of postmodernism to notice the staged suffering around them.

Most Berkeley students just want the degree. These days humanism was looked down upon as an empty metanarrative of the Enlightenment. Concern for the poor went out with the Aquarian Age and black-light posters. Post–Gen Xers were much too intelligent now to give financial support to the economically castrated, who'd just spend it on drugs, anyway.

Beyond the plaza, the campus wrapped its buildings around undulating lawns, murmuring brooks, old-growth trees, and pocket parks decorated with decent modern sculpture. It was a place to meander.

I stopped at spots to listen to the songbirds courting or to watch two squirrels running a barber pole course around an old redwood. Kidnappings, murder, potential imprisonment all faded into the background. The bees circling a nearby azalea bush were compelling enough to bring me peace.

I climbed to the top of a small hill. The path dropped down to Hearst Avenue. From this spot I could look right across a valley into the living room of my third-story apartment. The men going through my possessions were in clear sight.

Shit! Agent Dave got his warrant. Where was his evidence? Must have been the phone call from Louise to me just before she got bagged. Or those frigging shoes. Damn. Maybe it was the militia thing. Then I remembered something even worse. I hadn't turned the bookcase's back to the wall. In plain sight was a diagram of the murder scene, Max's surveillance reports, and reports from the Danville police database. I was utterly fucked.

So were Max and Sally. I wondered how long it would take the police to connect the empty envelopes with "#31" written on them with Northside Postal Services. I turned around and walked back down the hill in the direction I had come. When I was out of sight of my apartment window, I pulled out my cell and dialed Max.

I got Isabel. I said, "Tell Max that the FBI is searching my room right now, and they will find his reports." She said, "No problem," and hung up. No problem, my ass. Next I called Sally. She must have seen her caller ID, because she started talking as she picked the call up, "Hi. Sorry I was busier earlier today, big project had to get done in a narrow window. I got your message and I'm working on it. Some very interesting things popping up."

I said, "Houston, we have a problem."

"Uh-oh. Shoot."

I hoped no one was listening in. "They're tossing my place as we speak. They have your reports and the envelopes they came in. You better remove any tentacles you have into the station where those reports came from. They may be able to figure out the location where I received the packages. CYA time."

I could hear her fingers hitting the keyboard keys as I spoke. She said, "My ass is doing just fine. The situation you mentioned will be taken care of in the next five minutes. I hate to lose that asset, but I've got to. Right now I'm putting up my 'guards and wards' to keep any heat off of me. Hey, I'm sorry I didn't spot it sooner. Fucking feds. I guess you'll be hitting the road."

I said, "Are you kidding? I'm not leaving yet. We're on for our date this week. I'll see you there and then. I'm not the type to let a few law enforcement agencies cramp my style."

She chuckled. "You're all right, Nightrider. Don't come by. Use the red card in your wallet if you need to contact me. Bye till then, and be very careful."

"I will be. Peace, love, and understanding, baby," I said.

"Peace." She clicked off.

I noticed how calm I was. I had lived my whole adult life waiting for the knock on the door, the hand on the shoulder, the voice in the dark that told me I was under arrest. Ever since the sixties I'd been a fugitive, staying underground from both the police and my former radical comrades. This wasn't the first time I had to disappear, although this was as close as anyone had gotten to apprehending me.

I hoped my ancient history was still well buried. But even current events were enough to put me away for a while. Mine was not a life that could endure close scrutiny. Sooner or later they would uncover someone who would say, "Wait a minute, that's not Warren Ritter!"

I didn't know how much they knew. I knew my place looked suspicious. It would look even worse when they opened the black leather briefcase by the door. It held a short red wig, blue-colored contact lenses, a makeup kit, a Swiss Army knife, and $1,000 in twenties and fifties. Thank God I kept my passports in my storage lockup.

In a way, this couldn't happen to anyone better prepared. I'd leave my Honda where it was. It could sit there undetected for weeks on end. I got on the bus downtown and headed out to El Cerrito.

I got off on San Pablo and walked a half a block to Alfredo's Cycles. Alfredo took care of my Aprilia RSV Mille motorcycle. It had a fuel-injected 998 V-twin and was the fastest and smoothest bike I had ever owned. It put my former Ducati 900 SS to shame.

The bike was registered to David Ellbruck, my alternate Spokane identity. It was time to become Ellbruck for a while. I cleaned out all identifying information from my wallet and put

196

Warren Ritter's Nevada driver's license and credit cards in an envelope in Alfredo's safe. Then I opened the manila envelope marked "Ellbruck" and reloaded my wallet with his plastic and Washington State driver's license. I put on the leathers, driving gloves, and helmet that I also stored at Alfredo's shop. When I pulled out of there, I was a new guy.

There's something about wrapping my legs around 138 horses ready to leap forward at ninety miles an hour at the twist of my wrist that ignites a flame of freedom inside my gut. I headed for the freeway and just cranked it up for a while, whipping around cars, flying toward the city, and driving hard down the peninsula. The greed for speed. I just needed to feel alive! After a couple of hours of cranking it up, I realized it might not be such a good idea to get a traffic ticket right now, so I headed back to Berkeley.

I dropped by the bookstore where I stored my tarot stuff and paid them in cash for three months' storage. Next I headed over to the Rose Garden, a Victorian bed-and-breakfast. I rented a room for a week with my new name and new plastic. They were glad to give me a lovely tower room, with two exits and a good lookout over the road.

I had a couple of changes of clothes and a grooming kit in my saddlebags. I brought them up to my room. Sitting on the bed, I remembered reading about expatriate Israelis, who always had a bag near the door in case they had to go back home. My life had always been set up that way. It finally paid off.

I put my bags by the door, opened the yellow tablet on the sitting-room table, and positioned my chair so I could watch the front street. First I needed to clear my voice mail. There were three messages.

The first was from Jim McNally, my cop friend on the Berkeley force. He said, "Warren, I don't know what the hell's going down, but I just heard about the search warrant. I had to tell the force that we go shooting together. I told them how you hated twenty-two-caliber popguns, but the detective assigned to the homicide wasn't too impressed. He was much more interested in the fact that you're a crack shot. Sorry, guy. They're going after you, dude. They should have a warrant for your arrest in a couple of hours. Call me!" Cops make the best friends, the little stooge.

The second message was more direct. A Hispanic voice that I last heard in a cold, dark warehouse said, "You gettin' too close. Stay the fuck out of our business. Next time you're in Concord, watch your back, asshole." Somehow my chop shop buddies had tracked me down. More participants for the lynch mob. I began planning for a long trip north.

But the third call was the worst. Max was brief. "All surveillance is pulled. Our mutual zero-legged friend managed to wipe any trace of you off my computers just before the feds raided my office and confiscated every damn laptop. This sucks, buddy. I can't help you anymore. You're on your own."

Then I remembered Sally's emergency procedure.

I took out the red envelope that Sally gave me when this escapade began. I opened it and read the note inside, "If you're reading this, then everything has gone to hell. I will not be living in my house on Dollard St. I'll be accessing my hardware from a distance. Please do not enter that house. Anyone (besides me) who does so will regret it intensely. Call me as soon as you can and we'll coordinate whatever else needs coordination. I'm sorry for the inconvenience, but it beats prison for both of us. Sincerely, You Know Who."

Under the note was a column of numbers:

88732

2445

8119

I dialed 845-4223 and waited through the clicks. Sally answered, "This is Houston, come in."

I said, "Hey, lady, good to hear your voice. We're both domestically challenged right now."

"Not too challenging for me. I'm just a tad cautious when someone as close as you gets blown. Probably unnecessary, but I just can't seem to stop myself. Are you going to fade into the dust or hang around a while?"

"You keep asking me that. I don't think I need to vanish yet," I said. "If we can wrap this up in a couple of days, I'd like to stick around. But if this mess drags on, Berkeley might just be too hot for me this summer."

Sally laughed. "Oh, you Alaskan fishermen are all alike." How the hell had she found out about that job? That was ten years ago.

While I was battling off my paranoia, she went on talking, "Look, before I went on sabbatical, I spent five hundred dollars of your money. I have a friend who helped set up the computer system for the firm that's handling the beefy estate. I should be able to follow the money by tonight." Beefy estate, what the hell was that?

She went on, "Also, I did one last check before disengaging from our favorite station house. The prelim came in from the coroner. The bullet was a twenty-two, fired at almost point-blank range. Livor mortis evidence (whatever that is) shows Louise didn't die at the park. Her corpse was stored for at least four hours somewhere else. Time of death between ten P.M. Sunday and two A.M. Monday, depending on how hot it was where her body was stored. That's it in a nutshell. Anyway, call me around five. I've got to run, metaphorically speaking. Ciao, baby." Click.

CHAPTER THIRTY-TWO

I had just figured out that "beefy estate" meant Wellington and started to write "point-blank range" on my tablet when the other phone I carried around, Louise's cell, rang.

"Mom?"

Oh, my God, Heather was alive! Something inside me that had been dreading finding another dead body finally relaxed. I felt a tear touch the edge of my eye. I had to make sure she didn't hang up. "Heather, this is Warren Ritter, the guy you did the tarot reading with. I'm working with Louise to help rescue you. I can come and get you right now. Where are you?"

"I'm upstairs and the door and windows are all locked. I'm really weak." Her voice was strained, and she was whispering. "Can you really get me out of here right now?"

"Guaranteed. Tell me where you are."

"They're all quiet downstairs. It's too quiet. A while ago I thought I heard some shots. Then the TV got turned off. Now there's just somebody moving around. But I smell gasoline. I'm scared."

"Sure you're scared. Now go to a window and look out and tell me what you see." I didn't like that smell. Hurry up, Heather, don't get stupid on me!

"There's a top of a little store and the tiny asphalt backyard. It's a pretty big street out there. Lots of stores, kind of run-down."

God, this could be anywhere. "Anything unusual looking?"

"Well, way down the street, about halfway down the next block, I can see a wood-shingled kind of weird building. It's got a sign on it, "Ashkaz" or something.

"Ashkanaz?" I asked, but I already knew.

"Yeah, that's it. Where am I?"

I said, "Hang tough, Heather. You're still in Berkeley."

"Should I call the police?"

"You can if you want, but I'll get there faster, and I won't come in with sirens screaming and alert anyone who might still be downstairs. No one can get you out of there faster than I can, I promise you!"

"Okay, but hurry!"

"I'll be there in five minutes." I hung up.

She had to be on Tenth Street, near Gilman. Ashkanaz was a folk-dancing club, a community concert center, and hot spot for kicking off anti-imperialistic events.

I tore through the back streets on my bike with utter disregard for the speed limit. When I was a few blocks away from Gilman, screaming down Tenth, I saw a white pickup pull out from the curb on the next block and drive away. On a hunch I decided that would be the first house I checked out.

I knocked on the front door of a one-story green summer cottage. No answer. I looked through the front window. No drapes, no furniture. Deserted. I could see a taller house in the backyard. It looked high enough so that it might overlook San Pablo Avenue. Worth a try.

I dashed along the sidewalk that ran alongside the green cottage. Crammed into the backyard was a tall two-story box of a building that some greedy landowner slapped together to get two rental units onto one piece of property.

I knocked on the door. Nothing. I walked around the side. Drapes were drawn. The back door was locked, too. I was deciding that this was a complete bust when I smelled gasoline. Superhero time!

I took a couple of steps back, charged, and rammed my shoulder into the back door. Then I bounced off the door and fell over on my back. Damn, that hurt! It looks so easy in the movies. I started farther back this time and smashed into the door again. Nothing budged except me. I could break my collarbone this way.

Screw it! I grabbed a lawn chair and threw it through a back window. That worked much better. I was still wearing my driving gloves so it was fairly painless to break out the edges of the glass still stuck in the window frame and climb into the kitchen.

The room was a mess: pizza boxes and Chinese food containers piled up on the counters and crushed beer cans tossed on the floor. Dirty pans on the stove. It was a rat's heaven. The only oasis was the sink, which had a single clean glass standing in it.

The fumes were nauseating. My eyes watered. I grabbed a greasy towel to breathe through. With a towel over my face it was easy to trip over the body lying on the floor.

I fell to the floor and tipped a large bowl of gasoline all over my pants. My leathers were ruined.

Lying next to me was a dead woman. She was white, thin, somewhere in her forties. She had thick, peroxided blond hair, tiny blood vessels stretched across the surface of her cheeks, and a hole in the middle of her forehead.

As I struggled to rise, I bumped against a water balloon. It was hanging over my head, tacked on the edge of the dining-room table. When I looked closer I saw that it was a condom filled with liquid. A tiny hole had been pricked in the bottom and fluid was steadily dripping out. Around me were three large bowls of gasoline. No, four, counting the one I tipped over.

Wait a minute. I knew what this was. I'd read about this setup in a mystery book: *Watch Me* I think the title was. The heroine was an FBI agent assigned to a New Mexico arson unit. This was an arsonist's trigger. Inside that rubber was phosphorous, and when the water drained out it would be exposed to the air. Then it would burst into flame, and the gas would go up like the *Challenger*.

Sweat almost squirted out of my armpits. I'd nearly knocked that bulging thing on the floor, where it would have ignited. Right after that I'd have been kindling for a bonfire.

I wanted to run. I wanted to puke. Oddly enough, I did a brilliant thing instead. I reached up and held the rubber closed while carefully unpinning it from the table. Then just as carefully I lowered it into one of the bowls of gasoline until it was completely submerged. As long as the phosphorous didn't touch oxygen, it would not ignite. The trigger was defused.

I was safe. Or as safe as one can be in a fume-filled house, surrounded by bowls of gasoline and with fuel all over my right leg. Safety would end the instant an oven or a furnace pilot turned on, or a spark went off. I'd better find Heather and get out now.

I looked around. A mostly empty bottle of Chianti lay tipped over on the table next to half-full containers from a Thai restaurant. Underneath the stench of motor fuel I caught the rusty sweet smell of blood. Then I spotted another body, a black man lying on the couch. I walked over and saw a matching bullet wound in the back of his head. That's when I noticed the stairs.

They were carpeted in red with gold trim on the sides. Right out of my dream! But in the dream there was a kitten trapped upstairs. I was running up two steps at a time without thinking.

Four doors in the hallway. As I strode down the hall, I heard the muffled crying noises from behind the last one on the left. It was locked. No kitchen window to break this time. I was going to have to go through it.

I felt rage sweep through me. Fuck this guy! He wasn't getting Heather, too. I took three steps back and imagined that the door was not really there. I aimed my shoulder at a point two feet inside the room and drove toward it. The wood shattered around me. Cheap shit hollow-core door. I went flying through and fell onto the bed in front of me.

Heather was lying on it. Her trunk took most of the force of my body crashing onto her. She screamed. A man in gas-soaked black leathers had just flung himself on top of her.

I said, "Heather, it's me, Warren. I've come to get you. We've got to get out of here before the place explodes. Can you walk?"

She started to cry. I said, "Later for the crying! Get it together, girl. I need your help. Can you walk?"

She snuffled and then said, "I don't know. I've been in this bed almost all the time since they grabbed me. I crawled over to get my phone, and I pulled myself up to look out the window when I was talking to you, but then I had to lie back down. I'm pretty weak. Where are they? Are they going to kill me?"

I had to tell her part of it. I didn't want her falling apart when she saw them. "Two of them are dead on the floor downstairs."

"Did you do it?" she asked.

"I wish. No. Whoever is planning to blow up this house did it. We've got to get down those stairs. Help me out, now!"

She was still clutching her Eeyore cell phone. I looked around and saw her fanny pack lying in a corner of the room. She stood up. Her legs immediately collapsed. I caught her and braced her against my hip, and then dragged her over to the door. She dropped her phone and grabbed on to me. She could hold on to my shoulders pretty well but couldn't place much weight on her legs. But she was a tough bird. No more tears. It must have hurt like hell, but she bit her lip and held on tighter.

The stairs were a nightmare. We took them excruciatingly slowly. Three times we both nearly toppled over headfirst. Once we got to the first floor, I towed her to the front door. I unlocked it and, with her arms wrapped around my back, we made our way up the sidewalk to my bike.

She looked and smelled like a derelict homeless person. Therefore, she didn't attract any attention in the neighborhood we were in. I smelled like a Chevron station, which was a little more unusual.

After balancing her on the seat behind me, I started my bike. We heard sirens in the distance. I guess somebody called it in when they heard that kitchen window break. It took Berkeley's finest long enough to respond.

I drove away from the sounds of the sirens and pulled over behind the Chevron station. I briefed Heather on what I wanted her to say. Then I made a 911 cell call. I waited for the male voice to come on the line, "Nine-one-one, emergency services."

I handed the phone to Heather, and she said "This is Heather Wellington. Tell my boyfriend, Curtis Jackson, and my mom that I'm all right. A guy named Warren Ritter just rescued me from a house on Tenth Street in Berkeley. Two people held me prisoner there. When Warren came in to get me out of there, he found their bodies on the floor. A neighbor must have heard him break in. Police are on their way over there right now. Tell them to look out. There are bowls of gasoline all over the place. Inside one of the bowls is a condom filled with phosphorous. Warren told me to warn you to be careful with it. If it gets in the air, it will burst into flame. You better call the bomb squad." Then she disconnected.

Helmet laws are strictly enforced in this town. We swung by Alfredo's Cycles. Alfredo greeted me with, "Damn, man, you go swimming in the refinery?" I was not amused. "A helmet for the lady, Al. Put it on my tab, and hurry!" He did.

Then we went across town to my new digs. The back entrance was useful in this circumstance. I put one of the wicker chairs in the shower and told Heather to sit on it, undress, and get that B.O. stench off her. I left a T-shirt and a pair of drawstring pants of mine outside the shower stall.

I stripped off my petrol-scented clothes and put them out on the balcony. I wrapped one of the lush terry cloth robes that the B and B provided around me and waited until Heather called for help.

She came out, cleaned up and dressed in my clothes. She leaned against the door frame, looking like she was about to keel over.

Before she collapsed, I grabbed her and lay her down on my bed. Then I went into the bathroom and took her putrid clothing out to the balcony. Finally, I could get into that shower. The skin on my leg had already turned red from being soaked in gasoline. It felt so good just to stand under running water.

It was too soon to interrogate Heather. I put on my last change of clothes and came out with a smile on my face, "Hey, Heather, what do you want to eat?"

"A Big Mac, fries, and a Diet Coke. No, make that a big regular Coke."

Before I left to get her junk food, I had to tell her. I sure didn't want to. "Heather, your mother has been killed. Somebody shot her and dumped her in a park. No one has been caught yet."

Heather looked gray. She didn't cry. She just closed her eyes. I could hear her whisper, "Mom." She stopped listening to me, or even appearing to care if I was in the room or not. If I'd been Rose, I'd have had some brilliant question to get her talking. But I was pretty freaked out myself. I needed to go do something, not sit around and play therapist.

I said, "Okay, here's the deal. I'm going to go get us something to eat. I'm going to leave you my cell phone, but only on one condition. You don't call anyone but Curtis, okay? That includes your stepdad. We don't know who the bad guys are yet. If you need to get hold of me, I have your mom's phone. Deal?"

Again a whisper, "Deal." Rolling over, she turned her back to me and looked out the window. As I turned to leave, she said in a dead, flat voice, "Why did they make me write her a letter, telling her I was all right, and then kill her?" She kept staring at the nothing that was just outside the room.

She wasn't expecting an answer from me. "I'll see you soon!"

I said, and I was off again. I had to leave her a phone. If I took the cell phone she might use the one in the room. I didn't know who had done this, and I was scared that I might come back to a corpse.

I was back from McDonald's in fifteen minutes. She had fallen asleep on the bed, the cell phone beside her, right where I had left it.

"I'm hungry!" Her voice interrupted my nap. I uncoiled from the small couch I had curled up on.

I woke up with a rush of energy. It was time for the two of us to get moving. I knew that the cold greasy beef and soggy fries I had bought hours ago weren't the best idea for her first meal. I asked, "Are you up for a drive?"

"Sure, if you help me walk to the bike. I can hold on to you just fine."

Saul's Deli, smack in the heart of the Gourmet Ghetto of Berkeley, also had the best matzo ball soup in town. I took Heather out on a date. She looked like she loved it, the bike, the warm soup, and the relief of just being alive. God, after all this, she was smiling.

As we ate, we asked each other questions. She went first.

"Who killed my mother?"

"I don't know, but we're going to find out. My turn, now. Did you recognize anyone who grabbed you? Was it Hal or one of his gang?"

"No. I never saw them before, either one of them. About ten minutes after I left you on Telegraph, this salt-and-pepper couple in a white van pulled over and told me Curtis had been hit by a car. They said he was calling for me from his hospital bed.

Once I got into the van, the woman grabbed me and gagged me. How is Curtis?"

"He's fine, except that he's in deep shit. The cops want to pin all this on him. My turn. How the hell did you get a cell phone to call me?"

She smiled. "It must be that Eeyore phone cover. They must have thought it was a stuffed animal. Why didn't you want me to call the police to come get me?"

I had to play it honest. "The police think I did all this. I'm trying to find out who really killed your mom before they lock me up. I had to talk to you. My turn, now. Frank is your stepfather. What happened to your real father?"

Heather sighed, "My father was named Jerry Talbridge. Heather Talbridge is my real name. You remind me of him a little. Maybe it's the motorcycle. My dad was a tough little kid and ended up in juvie a couple of times. He probably would have joined the prison-industrial complex except that he met Mom. She straightened him right out and got him into commercial real estate and he made a bundle. He told me, the week before he died, 'Heathereen, I only got three pieces of advice for you. One, never turn your back on a friend when he's in need. Two, never trust lawyers or cops. And three, there ain't nothing you can't do if you want it bad enough.' My dad worshipped me. He died in a hit-and-run accident. They never caught the other driver."

Call me suspicious, but I didn't like the sound of that. "When did Frank get on the scene?"

"Oh, he was an old golf buddy of Dad's. He'd come over a couple of weekends a month when my dad was alive. When Dad died, Frank was right there for my mom, helping her out, doing errands for her. One thing turned into another, and pretty soon they were an item. Mom was really lonely, and Frank used to be really nice. Then, after he married her, he got surly, at least toward me."

I sat across the table from her in our booth and watched her as she talked. I noticed the changes from when we first met on Telegraph. She was thinner, with her cheekbones now clearly defined. The baby fat in her face had melted off. Something else had melted, some patina of innocence, naïveté, and childishness. I was sitting opposite a woman. A woman with dark shadows under her eyes. But no longer a girl. There was a determination that I had not seen when I first met her. She had gone through a personal fire and ended up tempered to a sharp edge. Strength looked good on her. This was no schoolgirl. She was an "up-and-walking" fine wench. I was damn proud of saving this one.

I finished the last bite of my pastrami sandwich, leaned back, and looked around. That's when it hit me. What the hell was I doing? Shit, I was wanted for murder. Cops were looking everywhere for me.

Here I was flirting with a girl half the age of my daughter while a manhunt was closing in on me. At any moment a Berkeley cop might wander in, recognize me, and arrest me. This tête-à-tête was a really stupid idea. Sometimes I hate it when I get manic. I completely lose my common sense.

Heather was surprised when I threw a twenty on the table and herded us back on the bike and into our nice anonymous helmets. Once we were rolling, everything was fine. I knew that, even with her on the back, this bike could leave any cop car far behind. My bike was just warming up when it broke ninety. So we went cruising. I took her up to Tilden Park. She rode beautifully, leaning with me as we blasted full tilt into those mountainous curves. It was a perfect rush. Whatever had happened to her in that Berkeley house had made her more fearless.

It was getting late. We swooped back to our tower room. I tucked her in bed and curled up on the couch. The lights had been off for about five minutes when I heard her say, "Warren, come here."

I was in my boxer shorts, so I wrapped the B and B's terry cloth robe around me and sat on the end of the bed.

Heather said, "I don't want to sleep alone tonight. Can you come in here with me?"

Oh, boy. This was a problem. "Sure," I said and crawled under the covers as far away from her as I could get.

She slid over. All she was wearing was my T-shirt. She wrapped one arm around me and then one leg around me, and lay with her head on my chest. She noticed my difficulty.

She said, "Do you want me to give you a blow job? I don't mind, really. Hell, it's the least I could do."

This reminded me of the sixties. Casual sex as a favor. I said, "I'm sorry, sweetie. That's a very generous offer. But I have a girlfriend and she wouldn't appreciate me taking you up on it." I had a girlfriend? Since when?

She said, "Okay, cool," and snuggled closer. I stroked her head. This little puppy had been through one holy hell of an experience.

It started almost imperceptibly at first. I felt the tears before I heard the sob. I kept stroking her, and more tears dripped down my chest. Soon she was sobbing deeply.

I held her close and said, "Yes, cry a lot. Crying is very good. Just let it all come out. I'm here. Come on, it's the best thing you can do." Stuff like that.

After about a half hour of sobbing, she was quiet, and then she began breathing deeply. She had just dropped off to sleep, switched off like a lightbulb. I lay there feeling the firm breasts of a young woman pressed against my side, smelling her hair that spread out across my chest. Sleep came much slower for me.

CHAPTER THIRTY-THREE

Heather had a deep night's sleep after her crying jag. She got out of bed in the morning and stretched unselfconsciously, like a cat. I enjoyed the view. Then she went in the bathroom for another shower. I got dressed and was ready when she came back out.

"Hungry!" she said.

"Let's do it," I replied. We walked down to the breakfast room and picked out a table on a glassed-in porch that overlooked the garden. She wolfed down a plate filled with pastries. I ate a bowl of raisin bran. Both of us drank pots of coffee.

While we ate, Heather told me her story, a very short story. "After those two grabbed me, they knocked me out with a shot of something. The next thing I knew I was strapped down to the bed where you found me. I never saw anyone besides the black guy and the blond. They kept me pretty well dosed all the time. After a while they stopped tying me down. I was too zonked to go anywhere. They would wake me up to feed me.

They'd walk me to the bathroom to use the toilet, and that's about it. No shower. It was gross!

"Occasionally I heard voices downstairs, but I never could make out who was talking or what they were saying. They weren't all that bright. They took my backpack but didn't check out my fanny pack at all. I guess they just opened it, saw Eeyore, and thought he was a Beanie Baby. They left the whole bag there in the room. Every so often they'd forget to drug me and I'd start to wake up, but I never got out of bed by myself until yesterday. I think they forgot to drug me. I woke up and could move a little. Then I smelled the gasoline. That's when I crawled over to my fanny pack, found the phone, and called Mom. But instead I got you." She looked down at her coffee and sighed.

I didn't want her sinking into grief again. I wanted her pissed. I said, "So, Heather, I'm going back to the question you asked me, 'Who killed my mother?' Now that we know that the two kidnappers were involved, both probably killed by the ringleader, it makes things worse. Hell, almost anyone could have masterminded these crimes. The three suspects I have are Hal, Frank, and Curtis."

Heather laughed. "Oh, I'm sorry. I didn't mean to be making fun of you. It's just that adding Curtis to that list is a joke. He's really nice and all, but at heart he's a teddy bear. I mean, he's a drama major, for Christ's sake!"

"Yeah, I know."

"How are we going to get the son of a bitch who did this?" Heather asked. She was ready for the hunt.

"Well, we need more brains. It's time for you to meet the rest of the team." I made a phone call, and Sally agreed to meet us at the wharf.

216

Berkeley's wharf was built in the early 1800s to onload wood, soap, gunpowder, and starch on the boats that went over to San Francisco. In those days it stretched out into the bay, well past the shallows of the shoreline, so that deep-draft sailing vessels could pick up and deliver freight. Most of the wharf had crumbled and fallen apart from disrepair, but a small section was still maintained by the city for lovers, families, and any fisherpersons crazy enough to eat the mercury-poisoned bay mutants that passed for fish.

Sally and Ripley met us in front of the restrooms at the foot of the wharf. Heather was a bit taken aback, especially by Ripley. Then Sally smiled. Heather turned to me and mouthed the word, "Girlfriend?" I nodded. Why not?

Ripley jumped up and began licking Heather's face, and her last fears were dissolved in dog spit. They chased each other back and forth as Sally and I made more sedate progress down the concrete-paved structure. Ah, youth.

I filled Sally in on the rescue. She said, "Yeah, I followed it on my scanner. The Bomb Squad was impressed with your damsel's precise directions. You probably saved a few lives there."

"Good. Enough people have died. Now, how are we going to flush out the real killer? We've been reacting while he keeps pulling all the strings. In aikido, the power comes from having the enemy come toward you. How can we get him moving in our direction?"

Sally told me her plan. I liked it. I rounded up Heather and her new canine bodyguard to see if she'd play along with it. We worked out exactly what we wanted Heather to say.

Sally got on her cell, and we listened as she talked to a friend of hers, a reporter for the *San Francisco Chronicle*. We put Heather on the line for the interview. Heather was brilliant. We'd make the front page tomorrow, for sure.

After the call, Sally invited Heather to spend the night with her. Heather was having a ball with Ripley. Heather looked over at me to make sure I didn't mind. No problem.

Just as well. Self-control lasts only so long. Sally was no fool.

CHAPTER THIRTY-FOUR

When I got back to my B and B, I checked my messages. There was just one, a message in Spanish. As far as I could make out, it was a man apologizing for dialing the wrong number. I recognized Max's voice and called Valdez Systems. I asked for Max. Isabel must have recognized my voice. She put me right through without asking for my name.

Max was brief. "Meet me in front of the house with the gnomes and don't be tailed. Forty-five minutes."

I set out on my bike. Sally's house was only ten minutes away, but it took a lot longer. Was someone on my tail? Was that the same navy blue Tercel behind me? If so, he must be pretty good, because I caught only a couple of glimpses of the car. Maybe I was getting weird. I no longer completely trusted myself. Was I losing it? What about dining out at Saul's yesterday? Stupid! I might as well just turn myself in.

I'd been too long on this manic upswing. Toward the top of

the arc, things can get a hard-edged paranoid tinge to them. But just to make sure, I parked a few blocks away from Sally's house. After twenty minutes of backtracking on foot, I was pretty certain that I was clean. I was just turning the corner toward Sally's when the passenger door of a brown Honda opened right in front of me and I heard Max say, "Get in." I did. He started driving. We both sat in silence for a few minutes while he watched his rearview mirror.

"Well, this is the best we can do," he finally said. "We're probably okay. Warren, I'm sorry. I hated pulling out from a case like that. You have some major federal heat on your ass, boy."

"No news there."

"Look, I had to take care of my people first. The reason I set up this meet has nothing to do with the kidnapping thing. I found your pregnant lady." He handed me a sealed white envelope. "All the information you need is right here. If you're a friend of Sally's you're a friend of mine. No charge. This is on me. You've been screwed enough this week."

How good a friend of Sally's was he? I was still mad at him, even though I knew why he pulled out. At least he was being pretty decent right now. And he was giving me my daughter! "Thanks, Max. Let me out here. See you later."

"Yeah, later."

I kept the envelope sealed until I was back in my room. I sat at the little desk and slowly opened it. I knew that what was inside would change my life. I read the three sheets of paper, reached for the phone, and then paused. I was going to have only one chance to do this right. I picked up a pen instead and began a note to my sister.

Dear Tara,

You said not to write a nice letter. So I will make this brief. My daugh-ter is named Francine Wilkins. Her husband is Orrin Wilkins. She lives at 42 Walk Circle in Santa Cruz. Her telephone number is 408-903-3343. The baby is due on June 14th.

I am not writing you this to show you how smart I am. I will not contact my daughter or let her know that I exist in any way, unless and until you decide that it is in her best interests to know about me. If you decide that it will never be right for her to know who I am, then I'll abide by that decision.

I have been thinking about what you told me. I can't expect you to trust me if I am not willing to trust you. I guess that's a small part of what you were talking about when you wrote about amends. I know it will take a long time. Let this be just a first step.

Your brother,
Richard

Now, back to the chase. I put the letter aside to mail later and pulled Special Agent Dave's card out of my wallet. I needed to know where the loyal opposition stood. How close were the cops to busting me? I used Louise Wellington's cell phone to call him.

"Yes, who is this?" What a friendly greeting.

I said, "Hi, Davie. This is your favorite practitioner of prophecy. Been sleeping well at nights?"

David said, "Look Ritter, I'm holding a warrant for your ar-rest. You need to come into any local police station and turn yourself in. Every day you're out there evading arrest, you make your case worse."

I was firm. "Oh, knock it off, Davemeister. You don't have a case. You have a personal vendetta. That was an illegal search of my home without probable cause, and you know it. There is no real evidence that links me with any of this. Just your vicious, unreasonable dislike. You are acting completely unprofessionally and are a disgrace to the bureau."

He said, "Dream on, mister. We have enough evidence to put you away for a long time. Your calling cards, a map of a crime scene that only the murderer could draw, the murder weapon, and other evidence that you can review in your trial!"

"What murder weapon?"

"The twenty-two you keep in your glove compartment. We found your car. Somebody had broken open your passenger window. It must have been one of your admirers, because he was nice enough not to take the gun. You're going down!"

Shit. Whoever was behind this was good. I had to give him that. How long had I been followed? But whoever it was didn't want me, he wanted a shot at planting evidence in my car. Even if I turned Heather over to them, Davie Boy would try to pin it on me. I had to settle this thing by myself. Nothing I could do but charge ahead.

I said, "Thanks, Davie. You'll have your murderer by tomorrow, and you can eat your goddamn warrant with Mendocino mustard."

I lay down to go to sleep. Not a chance. My mind started talking to me. *Warren,* it said, *you're wimping out. What a weak-assed letter. Crawling to your sister like a simpering little weasel. "Please, big sis, I'll be good! Now will you let me see my daughter?" What the fuck, it's your kid. No one has the right to get between a father and his child! Don't you have the guts to handle this like the true revolutionary Marxist that you are? Call Tara! Let her know how screwed up she really is. Tell her you're going to see your kid tomorrow,*

*and there's not a rat's ass thing she can do about it. Then call your little
girl and introduce yourself. Go ahead, show some balls! Thatta boy!*

I leaped out of bed and strode over to the phone. Enough
was enough! I was going to let Tara have it, both barrels. With
my other hand, almost outside of my own volition, I grabbed
my own wrist and stopped myself from dialing. I stood like that
for an instant, wrestling with myself. Then I collapsed into the
chair.

What the hell was I about to do? I could have blown any
chance of repairing the extensive damage I had caused. I would
have ended up alienating Tara *and* my daughter. I must be crazy!

That's when I finally got honest with myself about what had
been going on the past two weeks. I had been running on over-
drive, sleeping fitfully, making really bad decisions, and cogitat-
ing a mile a minute. I knew the warning signs well enough. My
fierce manic run was about to spin out of control.

That call would have really blown up in my face. It was almost as bad as the time back in Pelican, Alaska, when I drove the
mayor's car into the rotunda of the town library.

I had to stop myself! It was time to apply the pharmacologi-
cal air brakes. Immediately my mind reacted. *No, Warren, mellow
out. Go back to bed. Hey, after all, you didn't make the call. You're under control. Listen, buddy, you need this energy right now. Please, don't
turn off the magic!*

My manic voice always pleads with me when I decide to
start the medication. It always hurts to shut myself down. I felt
this aching grief at what I had to do. Mania is so expansive,
thrilling, and intense. It beats any drug, any sex, any pleasure you
can imagine. Just seeing so far, knowing so much, and riding
towering waves of energy was ecstatic beyond measure. Why
did I always have to crash on the jagged shoreline of practicality?

I got dressed and walked down to my bike. In a compartment set into the gas tank there was a bottle of pills, one of my
many emergency stashes. I swallowed a double dose of Depakote, dry. I needed big medical guns, and I needed them now.
Then I cranked her up. I laid scratch tearing out of that parking
lot. 232A Redwood Street, here I come. Look out, Hal. I was
going hunting.

CHAPTER THIRTY-FIVE

It was in a neighborhood of streets where tree roots buckled the pavement, driveways were clogged with rusting RVs, and front yards were cluttered with cars up on cement blocks. 232 Redwood was a run-down two-bedroom house behind a raggedy chain-link fence. A black Tercel was parked in the driveway. The house was dark, but a light shone from behind the garage. I hoped that was Hal's abode, or I was going to have trespassing added to my rap sheet.

I don't know what happens in normal people, but there comes a particular stage in some of my manic cycles where fear is completely eliminated as a motivator of behavior. I don't really care if I live or die, which really takes the teeth out of the mouth of death's dire wolf.

There was a curtain over the small glass window in the side door to the studio apartment behind the garage. I looked at the flimsy door handle. Remembering my embarrassment at bouncing off the door in the house where I rescued Heather, I centered myself and gathered my chi. Then, with a sideways heel strike, I shattered the lock and the door swung wide. Damn, why didn't I think of that last time?

I strolled past the wreckage of the hollow-core door and into the inner sanctum of my suspect. Hal was nude, stretched across his greasy sheets, and opening the drawer of his bed stand. I calmly walked toward him as he pulled out some sort of automatic and pointed it at me.

"What the fuck are you doing, motherfucker? Get the fuck out of here, before I fucking waste you!"

He had stood up, in all his naked glory, with his steel-gray penis substitute pointed at my chest. I looked down at the pistol. It was a Browning nine millimeter and he'd had the presence of mind to flick off the safety. Then I looked back up at his eyes. I let the silence hang there for a moment and then said, "Go ahead, shoot."

I watched the skin around his eyes tighten, and then his eyelashes twitched. Sweat started to glisten on his forehead. His gun wobbled a little.

I said, "I am going to reach out and take hold of your gun. Then I am going to drop it on the floor. Then we will either have a productive little chat or I will put out one of your eyes. Are you with me?"

"You make one move for me, motherfucker, and that will be the last move you ever make."

I slowly reached out, wrapped my fingers around the barrel of his pistol, and lifted it out of his grasp. There was no resistance. Then I dropped it. He jumped at the sound of the gun hitting the concrete floor. I reached over and gently pushed him. He fell backward into a sitting position on the side of his bed.

I stood over him. His pupils were very wide. "Where is Heather?" I asked.

"I don't know. You're the guy who sicced the cops on me. How the fuck do I know where that bitch is?"

He was getting braver. I reached out and placed the tips of my three middle fingers over one eye. He stopped breathing.

"Now listen carefully, Hal. I'm going to ask you one more time. If I don't believe you, I will be handing you your right eyeball. Do you believe me? Nod if you believe me."

He nodded and trembled.

"Where is Heather?"

He started to cry. I smelled a sharp odor. He had wet himself. He said, in a small voice, "I don't know, really I don't!"

I kicked his gun under his bed, turned around, and walked out. He was in the clear.

CHAPTER THIRTY-SIX

It was luxurious to wake up in the sunlight, finally relaxed. After my little lie detector test with Hal, I had come right back to my room and slept undisturbed by nightmares about bullet holes or red stairs.

Breakfast was Depakote with a caffeine chaser. It was a leisurely affair. I enjoyed reading the morning paper and politely ignored the other guests who filtered through the dining room. Our headline was quite satisfying. I was pleased until I read the ending.

DARING RESCUE ON TENTH STREET
Paul Jeffers, Chronicle Staff Writer

In a dramatic climax to the hottest story to hit the Bay Area in years, Heather Wellington was rescued from a house in the Berkeley flats just minutes before an incendiary bomb would have engulfed her in flames. In an exclusive interview with this reporter, she tells her story and brings us one step closer to capturing the mastermind of this kidnapping and murder.

Here is Heather's traumatic story in her very own words:

"I was tricked into getting into a van in Berkeley. A couple knocked me out, and when I woke up I was bound to a bed. I stayed drugged and tied down on that bed for seventeen days. Finally a man I knew saved me; he's an absolute hero. But he wants to remain anonymous. Anyway, he broke into the house and untied me. As we were leaving the house, he showed me the bomb that he had defused, which would have burned the whole place down. Also in that room were the bodies of the two people who had kidnapped me. They were both shot in the head. I'm lucky to be alive. I don't know for sure who did this, but I'm going to find out!"

The Danville police officer who is investigating Heather Wellington's kidnapping, Detective Robert Flemish, told us that the wine that was on the table of the living room of the house on Tenth Street was heavily laced with Rohypnol, the "date rape" drug. Whoever murdered the kidnappers drugged them first, then killed them. After that, he or she set a bomb to destroy the evidence and to destroy Heather in the process.

Detective Flemish also said that the man who rescued Heather was presumed to be Warren Ritter, a well-known sight on Telegraph Avenue. He is the local tarot card reader, who started his own investigation after doing a reading for Heather just before she was kidnapped. We have been unable to contact Mr. Ritter to comment on this story.

Turn to Page 3 for an in-depth analysis of these crimes.

I guess Flemish was paying back his debt. He was trying to get the Berkeley cops to take the heat off me, but now my cover was totally blown. I knew it was bound to happen sooner or later in this case. Now I was a public figure. Which would mean that, after I testified and helped put whoever did this away, I was going to have to move north and change identities again. Fuck! I'd worked so hard to disappear in plain sight on Telegraph, and now it was all undone.

But first things first. Whoever killed Louise was coming toward us now, I was sure of that. The only trick would be to nail him before he nailed us. I called Sally's new number on my cell. I got a weird recording. "Eight A.M. we three together will be where Ripley runs free."

I thought about it for a minute and then did the math. Ten this morning at Point Isabel Dog Park. The first time I did a reading at Sally's house she'd asked me to read the cards for Ripley, too: my first dog reading. When I got the Sun as Ripley's Significator card, Sally laughed. It is a picture of a joyous infant riding a huge stallion. Sally said, "That's Ripley at Point Isabel. It's a leash-free dog park on the shore of the bay. She's so crazy, wild, and free romping around those hills. I try to get out there at least once a week."

I had one thing to do before I took off. I was caught in a whirlwind of violence, and the last thing I needed right now was an hour of navel-gazing. I needed to cancel my therapy with Rose until this whole thing either blew over or blew up. I called her number to leave that message. I didn't get far.

"Rose Janeworth here."

I said, "Hi, Rose, I'm going to have to—"

She interrupted me, "Arnold, I've had enough of your crank calls. We ended our therapy six months ago. I still refuse to see you. I've given you a referral to a man who can help you. I will not take any more abuse from you, do you understand? Stop phoning me! The next time you try this harassment, I'm calling the police!" I heard the click of a disconnect.

Trouble in Kensington. There was no Arnold. This was a warning. The police must be hassling her, too. I'd better check this out. It was on my way to the park. I stuffed gloves into my back pocket, the ones I used in my one-evening-long career as a burglar. Then I put on my helmet, cranked up my bike, and headed for Rose's house. I figured that I'd be unrecognizable in this getup. As I cruised past her cottage, I spotted the fake PG&E truck on the corner. The workmen looked particularly listless. Rose's house was being staked out. They were waiting for me.

CHAPTER THIRTY-SEVEN

Sally's van pulled up in front of Mud Puppies, the doggie Laundromat at the park, just as I was locking my helmet to my bike. I was a little miffed at first to see the first person to get out of the passenger door. Max was dressed casually, Levi's and a windbreaker. You could barely make out the shape of the gun he was packing.

Heather erupted out the door next and came running over to give me a full-body hug. That was much better. "Oh, Warren, you'd love Sally's place. It's got a barn and a couple of horses, and its very own fishpond. So cool!"

Sally the farmer, another side I didn't know about. Next Ripley leaped over to French-kiss me. Then she and Heather started chasing each other. Max strode over as they went running toward the water. "Hi, Ritter. I'm playing bodyguard for Sally and her charge today. Good to see you."

I decided to take the stick out of my butt. I didn't need to be competitive with Max. Whatever relationship they used to have, Sally was with me now. I smiled and said, "Hi, Max. Good to see you. I'm glad you're on duty. I don't know what to expect today."

By then Sally came wheeling over. "Come here," she said. She reached up and took my face in her hand. I bent over and she gave me a very satisfying morning kiss. We started making our way toward the estuary, Heather and Ripley ranging out far ahead of us.

As she rolled along, Sally reached up and shook my hand. "Warren, you're the bomb. You asked the right question. It seems that the late Mrs. Wellington had an interesting clause in her will. She left her estate to her daughter, provided that her daughter survived her by more than six days. Otherwise it goes to her favorite charity, the Albany Psychic University. A hundred grand for her husband, but that's pretty much a token gesture on her seven-million-dollar estate.

"Then comes another interesting detail. Heather also has a will, made out last year. In it she leaves her estate to her parents if she dies. So, if she died more than six days after her mother died, her stepfather would be in line to inherit the whole enchilada."

"Damn," I said. "We finally found the greed. I *was* looking at everything upside down. It was Louise's murder that mattered, not Heather's kidnapping."

"Wait," said Sally, "there's more. I did financials on our three suspects. Curtis lives as a parasite off his parents' money. Hal probably does a cash-and-carry business because his bank accounts are extremely boring. But our friend Frankie Wellington has been drawing money out of his accounts in thousand-dollar chunks for months. He's almost broke, and his credit cards are maxed."

Heather and Ripley were sprinting toward us, Heather holding up a stick and Ripley jumping to grab it out of her hand. I said, "That son of a bitch. We're going to have to tell her. I don't think it's going to be a big surprise."

Heather tripped and fell. I was just about to yell out, "Watch it, clumsy!" when I heard Sally yell something. Then I saw a steadily growing red splotch in the middle of Heather's back. A bee flew right next to my right ear at the same time something hit me hard in the chest, and I went down.

CHAPTER THIRTY-EIGHT

The something that had hit me was a hundred pounds of black and tan attack dog. Ripley stopped standing on my chest on Sally's next command. Then I heard the sound of gunfire. Sally yelled, "Stay down, Warren. He's shooting at you, too." Ripley jumped off me, and I started crawling toward Heather's body. I looked over to see Max, crouched low, handgun pointed toward the marsh behind us. When I turned back toward Heather, Sally's chair blocked my path.

"Warren, get the hell out of here. I'm taking care of Heather. She's still alive. Remember, I was a medic. Max has the sniper running. You can't help here. Cops are going to be all over this park in five minutes. Now split!"

She had shoved herself out of her chair and was propped next to Heather's body, stanching the exit wound. She didn't have time to look up at me. I knew she was right. Hoping that Max was covering my back, I got up and sprinted toward the parking lot.

I jumped on my bike and slammed the helmet on my head. I laid scratch out of that lot. As I screamed onto the freeway, I saw police cars crossing the overpass toward Point Isabel. I pulled off at the university exit and headed for the wharf. I had to think, and act, very damn quickly or I was going to end up like Heather.

How did the shooter make us? He might have picked us up somehow at the wharf and followed Sally home. But that didn't make any sense. How could he have known about us meeting on the wharf? He had to be following me. I remembered the navy blue Tercel I thought was tailing me. But why didn't I spot him sooner? I suddenly had a very uneasy feeling. I got off my bike and began feeling under the mudguards. There it was, a transponder magnetically attached to the underside of my rear bumper.

I was tempted to toss it into the bay. But then a much better idea occurred to me. It was time for the hunted to become the hunter. I left it right where it was, got on my bike, and headed for Walnut Creek.

Nobody was tailing me by the time I got to Two Corte Real Plaza unless he was driving a Ferrari. It was not hard to find the silver Lexus with WELNGTN plates. I transplanted the bug from my bike to the inside of his rear bumper. Then I headed off to Antioch.

I drove too fast. I didn't dare slow down. The sight of that red stain spreading across Heather's back threatened to overwhelm me. I fishtailed to a stop in front of STORURSELF, punched in the security code, and when the gate opened drove to the office. I signed in as "Steve Warner." "Steve" paid his yearly rental fees in cash every January for a drive-in storage space, no questions asked.

My plan had been coalescing while I tore on out of there. There was a small blackboard next to the sign-in sheet, where clients could leave messages for the staff. I grabbed a piece of chalk from the tray. I was going to have a pressing need for it. I went to Number 154, unlocked the industrial padlock, rolled up the door, and wheeled my bike inside.

I turned on the light and pulled the door back down before unlocking the larger of two tall metal boxes in the back of the shed. I pulled down a case and unlocked it. There was my gun collection: five handguns, ten boxes of bullets, and a kit of cleaning equipment. I left the Kimber Team Match II in its velvet-lined case. It was the most accurate gun I owned, but the gun I needed right now had another, more valuable property.

The Smith & Wesson Model 19 Combat Magnum .357 had a six-inch barrel and no history. Supposedly a gun with this serial number was destroyed in a gun shop fire in Detroit in 1992. I bought it for five times its retail price, just in case someday I might need an untraceable piece. Someday had come.

After a thorough cleaning, I loaded it with hollow points, attached my Bianchi L-frame holster to my belt, and slid the revolver into place. Then I packed everything away and opened the smaller box. Inside was my safe. I spun the dial of the combination lock, opened it, and took out another $5,000. After tonight, I might be doing a lot of traveling. I locked everything away, pushed my bike outside, and pulled down the compartment door. Standing in the entryway, I looked up and down the long alley of locked storage shed doors. I was alone.

I'd never shot anyone. I knew that before tomorrow I would either be dead or I'd be a murderer. Or both. I hated *Dirty*

Harry. I refused to see action films, and I oppose capital punishment. On principle.

Someone without principles had executed three other people. Someone put a bullet in the back of my moral principles when he tried to take out Heather. I knew I had enough evidence to go to the police and get Frank arrested. I also knew that he had enough money to pull an O.J. and get off scotfree. Philip had told me that I was to be the instrument of justice. Now I understood. Standing alone in that empty street, I made my final decision.

First I had to set up this rendezvous. I stayed well under the speed limit as I drove back into Berkeley and headed into the hills above the university. I parked my bike out of sight around the back of the Lawrence Hall of Science and then climbed the hill behind the museum. I was set. Now it was time to "come to Daddy." I used Louise's cell phone to make the call. I tried to sound frightened. "Frank Wellington please. . . . Mr. Wellington, this is Warren Ritter, the tarot reader, remember? Look, something has gone terribly wrong. I think I got myself in the middle of something I have no business meddling with. I mean, I'm no Road Warrior. I'm just a simple fortune-teller, trying to mind my own business. Whatever is going on between you and your daughter is not my affair. I wash my hands of it. I just want to disappear into the woodwork. I really don't mean you any trouble. Can we get together and work something out here?"

In a neutral voice Frank said, "I'm not sure what you mean."

"I . . . I don't want to bother you or anything, but I think if we could get together someplace private, I could assure you that I am no threat to you or any plans you have. Maybe I could even help you out, if you know what I mean."

Again that chill voice. "No, I do not know what you mean."

"Okay, how about . . . Do you know where the Lawrence Hall of Science is in Berkeley? Up on the hill behind the university. Do you think you could meet me there tonight, at say seven o'clock? I will be at the big plaza in front of the hall. It closes at five so it should be pretty private up there at that hour. I'll be completely alone, really. I just want to get this thing over with. Maybe we can talk and work things out. Would that work for you?" God I was sniveling!

"Okay, I'll meet you then. Good-bye, Mr. Ritter." Click.

As I closed the cell phone I remembered a chilling line from Jean Anouilh's play *Antigone,* "The spring is wound up tight. It will uncoil of itself."

CHAPTER THIRTY-NINE

Is she dead?" I was calling Sally from my hunting blind.

"Critical. Still under the knife. No word from the surgeons."

"Shit. Sally, I'm going to have to take Frank out."

"I know. Scared?"

"Sick, scared, and pissed. I'll call later."

"Warren, good luck. And do me a favor, will you?"

"What?"

"Don't die tonight."

"A-OK, boss lady."

I put the phone in my pocket and sat back to wait. My life depended on my having figured this right, so I went through my reasoning one last time. Frank had hired a man and a woman to kidnap Heather. Then he must have hired someone else to kill Louise during the time he was setting up his alibi by calling the police. She was killed with a .22. The two dead kidnappers were probably also killed with a small-caliber gun. I saw the bullet holes in their heads, and those were no .357 magnum wounds.

Professional hits. Somebody put a .22 in my car, probably the murder weapon in all three homicides.

Bottom line, Frank must have hired a hit man. The same guy who took down Heather and made a try at me. If I was right, the sniper would be showing up any minute to find some high ground that looked over the Lawrence Hall of Science plaza. Then when I showed up at seven, he'd have me right in his crosshairs.

The view from where I sat, crouched down behind a stand of redwoods, rivaled the one out Rose's window. The sun had set, and fog had already rolled across the bay. It was filling up the basin that Berkeley lay in and would soon spill over onto the plaza right below me.

Lights illuminated the flagstones and the life-sized sculpture of a blue whale that stretched across the courtyard. It was a perfect place for a hit—open, deserted and well lit.

I watched the headlights of a car come around the last bend. It slowly turned into the drive that headed up to the Institute of Applied Sciences. As it passed in front of me, I saw one man driving a dark blue Tercel. Showtime.

I gave him ten minutes to find his roost. Then I cautiously made my way down the cliff from where I had concealed myself and headed up the drive, following the car. I walked very slowly, my crepe-soled shoes silent on the asphalt. I crept along the buildings, checking each parking lot for his car. In the last lot I found it parked under a tree.

From where the Tercel was parked, a small trail led down next to a clear patch of level ground. I slowed even more, watching where each foot went down, careful to avoid stepping on sticks, rocks, or gravel. I had plenty of time. I kept repeating a little mantra in my head, "I move silently and invisibly. Nobody knows I am here."

I spotted him in front of me and off to the left about fifteen feet away. He was lying prone, his rifle resting in the crook of his arm. He'd picked an excellent position, clear sight lines across the plaza but with enough low grass that he would be completely undetectable from below. He was talking on a cell. I unholstered my revolver and held it down by my side, waiting for him to end his call.

I was completely exposed, standing on the trail above him. All he had to do was twist around, and he could shoot me at almost point-blank range. But all his attention was focused on the killing ground below. Unfortunately for him, he was not psychic.

He flipped his cell phone closed and rolled into a shooting position, probably checking firing angles. I moved my gun into a two-handed shooting posture, legs spread, back straight. Fifteen, twenty feet, this was easy. I took bead on the back of his head. I seriously thought about just blowing him away right there. That was about as much fair play as he would have afforded me.

I had to live with this killing for the rest of my life. And unlike my opponent, I had a very well-developed sense of guilt. To assuage future self-recrimination, I had to give him a chance to surrender. That may sound foolish, but it wasn't completely insane. I figured we were pretty evenly matched. Sure, he's a pro. But I'm an excellent marksman. Big-caliber handguns were my weapon of choice. Let's rock and roll.

My hands were rock steady. I took three deep breaths. On the exhale of the next breath I said in a calm voice, "Drop the rifle."

He was very good. Catlike, he rolled left and then twisted,

swinging the rifle one-handed toward me like it was a pistol. I bet he could have planted a bullet in my forehead from that position.

However, I was expecting his move and direction. I aimed for the middle of his neck. A low-percentage shot, but I didn't know if he was wearing Kevlar body armor. He was erratically torquing his head, anticipating a head shot. His eyes just met mine when the slug I fired shattered his cervical vertebrae. He was dead instantly.

There's no silencing a revolver, so I just had to hope no one called that gunshot in to the police before I was finished with my work. I reached down and grabbed a handful of dirt from the path and poured it into my pants pocket. Then I tore ass up the path. It was 6:45 and I needed to get in position for my next visitor. I knew that Frank would wait to hear from his shooter. When no call came, he would have to investigate.

The evening fog poured over the wide, waist-high wall that enclosed the courtyard. I stood next to the stonework as the silver Lexus drove up to the front of the hall. I watched it stop. Suddenly the image of Maya, my aikido sensei, came into my head. She would stand in front of the line, short gray hair, fierce blue eyes, legs spread in a balanced stance. I could hear her crisp voice as she drilled us on the four purposes at the heart of aikido.

"In aikido, we learn to respond to any danger directed toward us from our centered place of integrity. Here are the four cornerstones of our work. One, we are able to perceive threats. Two, we respond naturally and instinctively to threats. Three, we redirect and neutralize the physical energy that our adversaries direct toward us. Finally four, we leave both ourselves and our attackers undamaged."

Well, Maya, I have numbers one, two, and three covered, but I'm afraid I'm about to royally violate the fourth principle. Frank got out, and I waved and used my submissive voice. "Mr. Wellington, I'm over here. I think we're all alone now. Come over here and let's talk." I was still playing the fool with him.

I kept both hands in sight. When he got within fifteen feet of me I spoke in a more forceful tone. "Stop, Frank, right there." He did. Both of us had our hands by our sides. I did not want a replay of the O.K. Corral. He hadn't drawn on me because he was waiting for his sharpshooter to take me out. It was time for my first little surprise.

"Look, we both have guns. I do want to talk to you, but I can't if I'm waiting every second for you to start shooting. Let's both move our hands very slowly, pull out our guns, and drop them on the ground."

Frank, very confident now that I had made yet another mistake, started moving his hands behind him. "Slower!" I yelled. He slowed down. Both of us pulled out our guns, bent over, and put them on the ground, with our eyes locked on each other. "Step away from your gun," I said in my most authoritarian, Highway Patrol voice. Frank took one step toward me and I took one step sideways, still keeping close to the wall behind me. If he had a second pistol in an ankle holster, I was a dead man.

"Why did you set me up?" I asked.

"None of your fucking business," Frank answered.

"I made it my business when I defused your little incendiary device and took Heather out of your two-story torch. And don't worry, you'll have plenty of time to answer my questions. Frank, you are about to join a long list of American presidents who discovered that it was a lot easier to get into a fight than it was to get out of it. We're going to have a little more time to chat than you planned, since the soul of your shooter is on his way to the innermost ring of Hades at this moment."

Frank's expression didn't change, but I could just make out some whiteness around his jaws. He was clenching his teeth. He said, "I don't know what you're talking about."

"Frank, you don't get it. This is not about the criminal justice system. I'm not wearing a wire. The police aren't going to jump out of the bushes and arrest you. I offed your goddamn hit man. That's what I'm talking about.

"This is personal. Pretty soon, one of us is going to kill the other. Now, you can talk to me or you can just make a move on me, but you're doing your own wet work tonight. Oh, and by the way, you'll be glad to know that Heather is doing fine. The bullet just grazed her shoulder. Your hired hand may be great at point-blank range with a popgun, but he sucks with a rifle. Now, I repeat my question, why did you set me up?"

Frank's temperature was going up. His face was getting redder and redder. I was counting on his temper. He started his prowl, inching closer and closer, speaking more loudly, building himself up to charge me. He was a tall, burly guy, and I'm sure he thought he could break me in half.

He growled, "You little weasel. This was purely a financial matter. It had nothing to do with you, you little shit. Why the hell didn't you keep your snout out of my business? You asked for it."

I just needed to egg him on a little more. "I get it, Frank. A capitalistic venture. Just good business sense. Invest in professional help and a little phosphorous. Implement a couple of terminations. Collect a seven-million-dollar return. What a big man you are, a real wheeler-dealer.

"You know, I was talking to Heather on the cell phone just

before I iced your boy, and she told me you tried to make a play for her once. But when she saw the size of your deformed, tiny little prick, all she could do was laugh."

Men are so predictable. He yelled and charged.

I thrust both my hands in front of me. Predictably, he grabbed at them to push them aside and throttle me. I raised my right arm over my head in a circular movement, pulling up his left arm in the process. At the same time I swung down my left hand, twisting him off balance. Then I stepped forward with my right leg and rammed my right knee outside his right leg. All I had to do was swing my upraised arm forward over his head and chop my left hand into his right knee.

If he were a fellow student at the dojo, his momentum would have swept him over my right knee. He would have landed a few feet away on his back, faceup on the mats. Instead he was swept over my right knee headfirst right into a cement wall. I heard the crunch of shattering neck bones. Frank's body convulsed once and then lay utterly still.

I rolled him over and put the back of my hand against his mouth. No air movement. I placed my fingers on his carotid artery. No pulse. He was a corpse. Louise was vindicated.

I made myself ice-cold inside. No room for feelings. Just do the next thing, and then the one after that. One step at a time.

The fog was swirling around us now, isolating us from the road. I put on the gloves in my back pocket. Then I walked over and picked up my .357, wiped it off, and knelt beside his body. I put the gun into Frank's flaccid right hand and pointed it toward the sky. Wrapping my finger around his, I fired off a round. Now his skin had some gunpowder residue on it.

Then I put that gun in his rear holster. I had enough adrenaline running in my bloodstream that it was no problem hoisting him up on the wide lip of the wall. I took some dirt from my pocket and rubbed it on the soles of his shoes.

I took out my piece of chalk and wrote on the wall, "I killed all of them. I'm sorry!" I crossed the "t" in "them" with that little affected tent top. I put the chalk in his right hand. Then I rolled Frank over the wall.

There was a silence and then a thump, the sound of a body falling two stories and smashing onto pavement. It was time to get my ass out of there. I picked his pistol off the flagstones and jammed it in my holster. Then I walked around the side of the hall to get my bike.

I drove back to the Rose Garden Bed-and-Breakfast and spent the next twenty minutes alternating between sobbing and throwing up in the toilet.

CHAPTER FORTY

It's horrible to kill people. Forget James Bond. Murder sucks. I was shaking and sweating. I kept washing my hands. I turned the TV up loud to get the sound of breaking bones out of my head. I started packing and then headed back into the bathroom to do more dry heaving.

I had to get moving. I changed my shoes, finished packing up my few toiletries, and used the room telephone to check my voice mail. Security didn't matter anymore. One call, my sister. Why was she calling? She couldn't have gotten my letter yet. "Richard, it's Tara. I guess I have some amends to make to you, too. I'm still infuriated at you, but my anger isn't helping my recovery any. My sponsor gave me hell for the way I handled you. Give me a month or so, and then we can get together and you can tell me what happened, back in '70. Just make sure it's the truth. It doesn't mean I'll forgive you. But I need to hear you out. I'll call you when I'm ready. Bye for now."

I could barely relate to her message. I was numb. All the stuff I felt about her seemed like it happened to someone else.

I checked the clock. God, it was only 9:30. It felt like 3 A.M. I called Rose.

She answered on the first ring.

"Can I come see you?"

"They left an hour ago. Come on over."

"Okay. I'll be there in half an hour."

I took my stuff down to my bike, along with two black trash bags I lifted from the wastebaskets. In one bag, I put my crepe-soled shoes, Frank's semiautomatic, and my "burglar" gloves. In the other I stuffed Heather's smelly clothing and my gas-soaked leathers. Then I knotted the bags and poked a few holes in them. I drove to the wharf. It was deserted. No one saw me throw the bags into the fog. They landed so far away I could barely hear the splash.

Then I pulled out my cell. I was afraid. I really didn't want to know. I hit redial.

Sally answered, "Warren?"

"Alive and kicking. How's she doing?"

"Thank God you're okay. They took her back into surgery fifteen minutes ago. I told the nurse I was her sister, so he let me know that her condition is still very critical. He said, 'If she really wants to live, there's a small chance she might make it.' That's all I know. I'm so glad you're alive. I wasn't ready to lose both of you tonight. What happened?"

"They're gone. Totaled. I don't want to talk about it."

"So now what happens to you? Are you taking off? Will I ever hear from you again?" Her voice was matter-of-fact. She sounded already resigned.

"I don't know. I've got to get out of here, that's for sure. I'll call you when I can."

Again she spoke in a neutral, sad voice. "You're a runner,

Warren. I should have known better than to let you in. Go on, do what you need to do. But I changed my mind. Grant me one last favor. Please don't call me again. It's hard enough. Good-bye, Warren."

I said, "Good-bye Sally," but I think she had already disconnected.

CHAPTER FORTY-ONE

I t's all very convenient, isn't it?" Rose asked.

She had greeted me at the side door in a long, flowing dress covered with dark purple roses. But she hadn't had time to do her makeup. Her eyes looked tired.

I told her everything that had erupted in the past twenty-four hours. She listened, still and neutral. When she said, "You've been through hell," I started to cry. Then I yanked myself together.

Rose asked, "So, what's next?"

"I'm out of here. Time to fly away. I staged Wellington's murder like a suicide, but I don't think it'll fool anybody. The cops were in my pad. Now they have my prints and DNA. They'll find some trace evidence leading to me. Some frigging reporter is going to take a picture of me. Somewhere, someone is going to put it all together and say, "He's still alive." Then they'll come after me. I've gotta split. I'll miss you, Rose."

That's when she made the crack about how convenient it all was.

"What do you mean?"

"Well, you never have to worry about getting too close to anyone, do you? Every five years or so you pull up roots and disappear without a trace. All for very good reasons, mind you. What were some of the ones you told me? An aggressive IRS audit, a violent attack from one of your old bomb-throwing buddies, the auto crash in Alaska, and that mess with the hooker and her pimp.

"Eight years, this is the longest you have ever stayed in one place since you started to run thirty years ago. And now you have excellent reasons to 'fly away,' as you put it: kidnapping, murders, manhunts, nationwide publicity."

"Look, Rose, I don't know what you're implying, but I have no intention of spending the rest of my life in jail, thank you very much!"

She was unruffled, as usual. "You also have a less savory reason for leaving, don't you?"

"I don't know what you mean."

Rose smiled a humorless smile. Her voice was ice. "Let's start with me. I know you haven't told me everything. There's something that happened to you to start this flight that you hold very close to your chest. But I probably know more about you than anyone else on the planet. I represent a large threat to your need for secrecy. When you leave, that threat will end."

"Don't get a big head," I said. "I'm not doing this to run away from you."

"Not *just* me," Rose replied. "There are a few other people. You almost fell in love, a vulnerability that a man on the run cannot afford. You saved someone's life, a girl who cares a lot about you. You've met your sister, which could bring up all sorts of unpleasant emotions of guilt, shame, and longing. You have a daughter who's about to give birth to your grandchild. A grandfather! That surely doesn't fit your image as Easy Rider."

I didn't like this conversation at all. "Get to the point, Rose."

"Warren, I'll put it to you straight. This story you tell yourself about needing to run in order to protect yourself is a lie. You keep telling it to yourself so that you don't have to face the truth. You're afraid of growing up.

"No one is going to stop you from running, except yourself. You continue to atone for some sin that you committed thirty years ago. You destroy yourself by repeatedly erasing your identity. But all that sacrifice is never going to bring you peace. It only brings a painful detachment from the richness of life. You're terrified of stopping long enough to care deeply about another human being.

"Look, Warren, life has nothing to do with playing it safe. Life is filled with angry sisters, disappointed lovers, hurt daughters, pushy therapists, suspicious cops, and one messy situation after another. Maybe it's time you stayed around to clean up some of those messes. It may be dangerous, and I guarantee it will challenge every bit of stamina and courage you possess, but that's what it takes to grow up."

For the first time in our work together, I got up and walked out. I wasn't angry at Rose. Well, actually I was angry at Rose. But I was also feeling too lost to stay another moment with her.

I was done. It was time to leave town. I could leave the crap in the apartment behind. I had credit cards and a fast bike. Time for a new start. I was out of here.

CHAPTER FORTY-TWO

I drove my bike across the bridge to San Francisco. The fog was socked in heavy, just the way I loved it best. I whipped through downtown and out to the avenues. One last look at the Pacific and then on the road. I dead-ended at Ocean Beach. I'd gone as far as I could go in that direction. There was no place west of here. I could go south and spend summer in Belize. I could go north and become Dave or Ray. Or I could go back home to skeptical cops, hungry reporters, a disappointed lover, a dying girl, and an unknown daughter. I wasn't sure which direction I was going to choose. I got off my bike, took off my helmet, and sat.

A wave washed in and slid across that long, dirty stretch of sand where San Francisco plunged into the sea. I squatted on a concrete wall, fog cloaking me.

The next wave broke, growling at me. It wasn't loud enough to drown out that horrible noise. I couldn't get the sound unstuck from my memory: a crunch like a dog biting a bone in half, the crack of a man's neck breaking. I wanted the smell to go away, too. I'd washed my hands with Lava soap fourteen times since I'd pulled the trigger. My skin was raw. It didn't matter. In my mind I still reeked of gunpowder.

I listened as the dirty water hissed its way back out to sea. I wanted a way out, too. Next to me I heard a *ping* from my motorcycle. The engine block was beginning to cool from contact with the thick mist. I needed to fire it back up. Take off, full throttle. Corner so hard my knees scraped the asphalt and then scream down the highway at one twenty. Gone, without a trace.

Behind me the slick suck of tires on the Great Highway kept time with the surging breakers. Fog wrapped its private arms around me. I was finally removed from the world of hit men and heartbreaks. I was on my own little island, bounded by the circumference of my vision, suspended between the ceaseless pulse of the sea and the migratory call of cars passing in the night. I thought about the past three weeks. I asked myself, *What the hell happened to me?*

The image of the Eight of Swords came back to me. That didn't just stand for Heather, tied up on her kidnapper's bed. That was me, too, blindfolded by my anxiety and trapped in a cage of swords. I could ride forever on my fancy motorcycle, but I was incapable of staying around to love and trust somebody. My heart was held captive to my fear.

A slide show started in my head. First came Rose, thin lipped and in my face. The next picture was Tara, in that one moment on the Ave when she smiled and I felt how much I missed her. Then a hazy pastel-smeared slide of my daughter holding her child. The memory of Heather followed, eyes still wet, asleep on my chest. Finally, Sally smiling, my high priestess. Philip had laid it out for me, back on Telegraph: a choice point, a crossroad. I could choose another thirty years on the road, or something completely dangerous and unknown.

I was fifty-five years old. I shot straighter than most cops, rode harder than most kids, and I'd stayed underground and free for thirty years. It took less than a month to unravel all that. Now, all I wanted to do was run. And I couldn't. I'd changed. I couldn't get it up to take off again. I didn't know what to do. But I wanted the run to end. I wanted a lot of things. Most of all I wanted someone to care that I stayed around.

I pulled out my cell and hit redial. Hers was the last number I'd called.

Sally said, "What do *you* want?"

I took a deep breath and said, "Hey, Houston, I have a problem. I want to run, real bad. I'm scared as shit of you, Berkeley, Heather dying, everything. I'm so afraid I'm going to get busted and tossed in jail. I want to break free and ride forever. But I can't just take off this time. My goddamn heart won't let me. I don't know how to stick around. Will you help me?"

THOMAS DUNNE BOOKS.
An imprint of St. Martin's Press.

www.minotaurbooks.com

Library of Congress Cataloging-in-Publication Data

Skibbins, David.
Eight of swords / David Skibbins.—1st ed.
p. cm.

ISBN 0-312-33906-2
EAN 978-0312-33906-7
1. Tarot—Fiction. 2. Fortune tellers—Fiction. 3. San Francisco (Calif.)—
Fiction. 4. Identity (Psychology)—Fiction. 5. Psychological fiction. I. Title.

PS3619.K55E53 2005
813'.6—dc22

2004059028

First Edition: April 2005

10 9 8 7 6 5 4 3 2 1

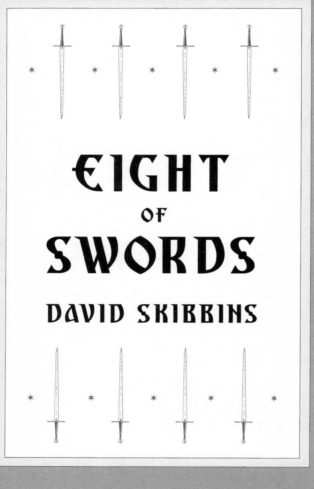

€IGHT

OF

SWORDS

DAVID SKIBBINS

THOMAS DUNNE BOOKS
ST. MARTIN'S MINOTAUR
NEW YORK